William Clark Russell

A Tale of Two Tunnels

A Romance of the Western Waters

William Clark Russell

A Tale of Two Tunnels
A Romance of the Western Waters

ISBN/EAN: 9783744777179

Printed in Europe, USA, Canada, Australia, Japan

Cover: Foto ©Andreas Hilbeck / pixelio.de

More available books at **www.hansebooks.com**

A TALE OF TWO TUNNELS

A ROMANCE OF THE WESTERN WATERS

BY

W. CLARK RUSSELL

AUTHOR OF

'THE WRECK OF THE GROSVENOR,' 'THE CONVICT SHIP,' ETC.

A NEW EDITION

LONDON

CHATTO & WINDUS

1899

CONTENTS

A TALE OF TWO TUNNELS

CHAPTER I.

THE DEVIL'S WALK.

THE ship *Lovelace* lay in the East India Docks, being newly arrived from an East India voyage. Her commander, Jackman, stood in her cabin and gazed in his glass; he looked at his face, and seemed to study it. There was a mark as of a blow close under the left eye, and he examined this mark with care.

He was a handsome man, with regular features and a dark brown skin. His eyes were black and flashing, and, contrary to the custom of that age, he wore his hair close cropped behind. Being satisfied, he picked up a bag, locked a drawer, quitted

I

his cabin, withdrew the key, and left the ship.

He made his way on foot and by coach to Cannon Street, where the offices of the owners of the vessel were situated. Just when he was in the middle of the thorough-fare he was knocked down and his bag taken from him. He lay stunned for some moments, and, when he sprang to his feet, he caught sight of the darting figure of a man flinging the bag into some wide area and rushing on.

Captain Jackman gave chase, but did not somehow think of recovering his bag. Then, feeling confused and amazingly shocked by this theft of fifteen hundred pounds in gold and paper—mostly in gold—the money of the owners, he gave up, and walked sullenly, without even thinking of brushing his clothes, towards the offices.

Such was the story related to the owners by Captain Jackman of the ship *Lovelace*. He said he believed his assailant was a rascally little seaman whom he had shipped at Calcutta, and who had given him trouble all the way home.

Did Captain Jackman see the man?

Yes. Just outline enough of the flying figure to guess that it was he.

How was the money done up?

In three small bags.

Would he have had time to take these parcels out of the captain's bag in the narrow compass of time allotted him by the narrative?

Certainly. He had himself seen the sailor fling the bag down the area. Sailors are swift in breaking bulk. Some are born thieves. This sailor was peculiarly active, and was the one of the whole crew, knowing that Captain Jackman was going to carry a large sum of gold ashore, to rob him out of hand.

'How did he know that you were going to carry a large sum of gold ashore?'

'It may have leaked out through my servant, who, being a neat hand, packed the money for me.'

They went to the police. They searched the area, and found the bag, but they did not find the gold. What, then, was to be done? Raise a hue and cry?

Captain Jackman was grimly regarded by his owners, who had lost in Cannon Street a very handsome venture in their voyage.

'I hope,' said the captain, when he called at the office two days after the incident, 'that this will not make any difference in our relations, gentlemen.'

'You shall hear from us, sir,' answered one of the owners, a tall lean man with a dangling eyeglass, bending his form crane-like towards Jackman. The captain seemed to pause, to look confused and pained. He then, with a polite bow, raised his cap and left the place.

'I noticed a rather ugly mark near his eye,' said one of the partners. 'Ay,' said the other, 'and plenty of dust in his clothes.'

One day, some mornings after this, a fine young woman was pacing the sands of the sea-shore, lost in thought. The sands formed a noble stretch of promenade, brown and beautiful with ripples moulded by the waters of the sea. But from the wash of the surf the brine was sparkling and flashing : it was blowing half a gale. The tall, mid-Channel combers raced inshore, following one another like cliffs looking over cliffs. The girl's dress to windward blew to her figure, and showed her a beauty in shape : sometimes she paused, and turned to look at the sea, which swept into hilly heights of froth and obscured the horizon by miles of dazzle. Also, she took notice of a little barque staggering down Channel under close-reefed sail, sometimes vanishing, and then showing her whole shape. The sight was so toy-like, it made one linger. All the wet glories which came out of the sea with that little leaning, flying fabric glowed in each sparkling sunbeam that touched her. She was quaint, too, as an example of a vanished type of ship, though she belonged to her age. She was very high in the stern —a pink—and her bowsprit ran up like a mast. Her topsails, when set, would have a curiously lofty hoist for a vessel of her size. Such as she was, there she was, all of the olden time, spinning through the blue marrow of the Channel, and making for some far western port.

All on the left of the young lady rose a towering terrace of cliff, white and gray blocks, seared, ravaged, scowling, menacing the up-looker with the headlong threat of its topmost reefs. It went for miles. At some distance its curvature frames what is now a well-known watering-place.

The narrative must stop an instant to describe the young lady. Who is this girl that is walking solitary along the sands under a great height of cliff before the midday dinner-hour? She shall be introduced at once as Ada Conway, the daughter of Commander Conway, R.N., a gentleman of spirit, who had seen service, who lived in a comfortable little house out of eyeshot of the wash of ebb-tide. She was a tall girl, above the middle stature, of mould in absolute proportion. She had thick black hair. She was Eastern in her colour and eyes, yet had as fine a type of English face as you could wish to see. She was dressed somewhat quaintly in a sort of turban hat, with a short ornament of feather or bird's wing buckled to it by a fal-lal in gold. Her dress was of green material, and was cut so short-waisted as to reach nearly under her arms, where it was clasped in a girdle. This early century beauty blew along athwart the shrill gale and over the ribbed brown sand. And sometimes she looked at the leaning barque, and sometimes she stopped in earnest to take in the whole sumptuous mass of mountainous breaker, lifting into Atlantic height, before falling with the dead crash of the defeated billow.

Suddenly her ear was caught by a sound proceeding from the direction of the cliff. It did not come from the base; it did not come from the summit; but, womanlike, she must needs look along both. She was passing on, when the same strange, alarming cry stopped her, and now she had the good sense to scan the front of the cliff, where might-be she should see a man hanging by his eyelids to the edge of a rock, or some helpless boy in a hollow, lowered thence by a bowline, and lost to recovery by his friends.

The terrace of cliff was a vast expanse of holes and fissures—great crevices of the size of gaps; it buttressed out in parts with natural effect, was solid and green at its base, and was a noble example of an English sea-board. Miss Conway directed her eyes over the face of the cliff very carefully, studiously, as of purpose, under her shaded hand, missing the hole from which the voice was proceeding. She then, with a start, beheld a part of the figure of a man standing in a hollow of the cliff, well known to her, as a young lady residing in those parts, as the orifice of a smuggler's tunnel called the Devil's Walk.

She saw him wave a handkerchief. She pulled out hers and waved it in return, running a little way towards the base of the cliff, and shrieking—-

'I know where you have got fixed. I will release you !'

The wind carried her high and powerful notes. The man in the hole flourished his arm with the most cordial, grateful gesticulation, and the young lady walked swiftly towards the little town which lay in an embrasure in the great cliff on her right.

The road was steep, wide, and formed an angle. It went like a steeple into the sky.

People often paused to admire the gulls floating round about and in and out the liquid blue of this fanciful aerial spire. Nothing of the town was visible till almost the summit of the great gap had been reached, when there began to steal upon the sight a row of little houses built of flint, further off a church, then again a pleasant little rectory-house. Houses broke the landscape, which had few trees, and was hilly only in the distance. It was a sort of town that seemed to have settled down to nothing and to seem nothing. It gave itself no airs ; all was chaste and sober—of a Quaker-like trimness of aspect. In a small garden, distant by about a mile from the bulk of the town, stood a cottage of two stories, square and strong for the gales. It was Commander Conway's home, and the home of his daughter Ada. The girl went swiftly along the edge of the cliff, this time towards the right. She had come about a mile along the sands ; she had now to retrace her steps on top. It was not very strange that she should know exactly where the man was imprisoned. She had lived many years in those parts, and knew most of the traditions of the smugglers, and had grown acquainted with their haunts, and had visited them, through talking with old sailors to whom times were always hard. How distant the rolling blue sea seemed all that way off! A full-rigged ship was then in sight, looking close in; she rolled in the noblest majesty the deep can clothe her toys with.

But Ada had no eyes for pictures of the sea or sky, for processions of clouds, nor ear for the gull screeching in its soft white plenty midway high, nor for the breaker arching like glass to the sand. Not just then, anyhow. She struck a path, and walked with vigour about a mile, deviating into a part of the land, about a third of a mile from the brink of the cliff.

She arrived at a strange old enclosure. It might have been some ancient smuggler's vault, the memorial gone, nothing but the flat tombstone and the square of broken neg-lected railings left. She squeezed through these broken railings, and approached the small flat stone, which was fitted with a ring in the middle; but this she had known for years. Not a living creature was in sight, not even a goat. That vast down of cliff swelled its rampart without visible figure of man to the distant hills.

It seemed a desolate scene even now. One might figure it with some sense of horror in a gale of wind black with snow, so dark that if you did not mind, the next step might carry you into the scaling hiss that was washing, bubbling, fretting, trumpeting into breakers just below.

Miss Conway seized the ring and raised it, not without exerting considerable strength. She had often raised that stone cover, and now, when she had got it off, she knew what to do. It was, in short, the entrance to a smuggler's passage, designed for the lifting of goods from a height. It had been abandoned, not, however, before it had been formed, nor before a whole wheel of like corridors had radiated out of this mainspring under the earth. All were of no use, and had been deserted by the smugglers as worthless. Few took much trouble to wander in those cold caves. They felt tolerably certain that bold Bill and Harry

Spikem had not left anything worth their acceptance in those gloomy depths. Boatmen offered to conduct visitors through them for sixpence ; but a visitor was an extremely rare bird at a town where there were no lodgings to be had, and but two small inns of those old days for the traveller to put up at—inns such as Nelson sat in with Collingwood and his wife in a little room, whilst little Miss Collingwood watched the dog playing.

The stone being lifted, Miss Conway peered down and called. She peered down and shrieked. The echoes of her voice seemed to flash like light, so piercing were her tones. But under earth the voice is very deceptive, as you shall know if you hail a man from a depth of soil.

Why couldn't he have come to the place where he entered ? she thought ; and then she reflected that he might have strayed in one of the corridors, and have got to the end of it, and was there standing, thinking the entrance was over his head, and waiting with a beating heart for his release. For certain it was there was no release for the man save through the smuggler's exit.

If that was his luck in those branching corridors, he would have been well off had he fallen and been caught by some projection of rock; for then they could have seen him above; they could have lowered tackles and a bowline; they could more clearly have heard his shouts. Now he could not approach the seaward-facing hole so as even to show himself to those down-looking.

A flight of four rude steps sank into the gloom, and the cutting went away in blackness. She had a great deal of pluck in her veins; only a plucky woman, single-handed, would have ventured this rescue. It was no longer now like opening a trap-door and letting a man out; it was seeking for a captive in blinding blackness, save where the orifice in the cliff let in at its mouth of tunnel, at a distance, a green light like the object-glass of a telescope at evening.

It was clear that some officious hand must have closed this trap-door above on observing it opened, supposing it so by neglect;

for the people of the place, though they got
no money by the thing, rather valued themselves upon it as a small sight, though there
were scores of greater wonders, east and
west, particularly west, much of the same
kind. Ada walked a little distance, until
she was plunged in darkness ; she then stood
and shouted—

' Where are you ?'

No answer was returned. Some faint
sheen from the trap-door lay just here, and
a little further onwards, and you could have
distinguished the marks of the axe in the
solid stuff the dare - devils had sheered
through till they came to the open. The
labour was wonderful because it had been
secret, it had been done in passages of blackness in long nights, with look-outs to silence
the axe and hands striking fiercely, by small
lantern light, against the portion they had
opened by a line ruled straight by magnetic
compass.

But Miss Conway knew that the smugglers
had run a number of tunnels, besides this
long corridor, on either hand of it, extending
like the antennæ of an aquatic insect. If

the man had wandered into one of them, then, after she had cried aloud in vain to and from the central passage, she must return for help and lights, and make a proper search.

She walked on, again paused, shrieking in her singing, ringing voice—

'Who are you who have been caught down here?'

This, however, did not last long. She had neared the orifice overlooking the sea—close to, it glowed like a lamp in the cliff side—when her cry was echoed in a loud note, and a man's shape stood between her and the light.

'Oh, there you are!' shouted the girl, greatly relieved. 'I was afraid you had got lost in one of the off avenues.'

'You are extremely kind to come to my help,' he exclaimed, approaching her.

She could clearly see the movements of his shape against the disc that shone behind him.

'I don't know what I should have done. I don't know how long I've been locked up. I am very hungry, and could drink a gallon of beer.   Was not I an idiot to come into this place?'

'I think you were,' she said.   'Did you pull the stone up?'

'Yes,' he answered, 'and some villain seeing me descend must have sneaked to the pit and put the stone on, for when I returned, making sure of my exit by that lighted hole yonder, lo! there was no light; all was blackness.   I was without a stick, without means to knock upon it.   Good heavens! what was I to do?   There was only one way out, and that was over the cliff, about eighty feet of fall, as I took it.'

'What brought you here?'

'Curiosity, and,' said he, laughing, 'an inborn love of booty.   I had read in my time a great deal of the old smugglers—of their shifts and ways—and knew that this and the adjacent coast contained many of their caves.   I got a plan of this one from a man in your town, and entered it with a candle, and explored by candlelight; but the candle burnt out long ago.   Idiot-like, I dreamt of run goods neglected, of hard specie in canvas, and tobacco in wood.'

'You never find such things,' said the girl, 'in our caves—the men were too cunning. They did not work for you or for me.'

'Pray what time is it ?'

'About noon.'

'Lord! then I have been here since four o'clock yesterday afternoon !'

'It is time we got out,' she exclaimed. 'Did never a man pass below in so many hours ?'

'Two shrimpers only did I see far out— aged, bowed shapes; and I could not have made myself heard.'

'Now hook your hand into this pleat,' said she, taking his hand and fixing his finger for him.

They walked in darkness. It never will be known how it happened—whether Miss Conway had, in that moment of excitement, failed to take a glance at the wall-star at the end, and turned with her companion into one of the long out-leading corridors, or whether she had absolutely forgotten her geography of the place in the blackness that was upon them, for she had never contem-

plated passing more than a few steps beyond
the entrance to the cave.   She grew sensible
of her blunder when they arrived at the extremity of the cutting, which had, doubtless,
other avenues forking out of it.

'I believe,' she cried, in a low voice, 'I
have mistaken our cell.'

'In the name of mercy don't call it a
cell!' he exclaimed, with the very presence
of a shudder in his speech. 'In the long
hours that I have been haunting these holes
like a worm I have seen sights, and I have
heard sounds, and amongst the sounds I
heard was the faint, everlasting crying of the
dead for those they loved, passing through
the earth.'

'This is no place for such talk,' she
exclaimed, baffled by the blindness of the
cave.

They returned, still linked, but somewhat
ironically.   It seemed certain now that they
took a turning to the left, for they missed
the star, and came against the blank wall of
the cliff, as they supposed.   Strong of heart
as was the girl, she was beginning to grow
frightened; nor was there any consolation

to be found in the idea of her having a
companion and a protector.   Who was he?
Well, so far as his utterance could pronounce
him, he was a gentleman, gatherable from
his speech, of a somewhat heedless cast of
mind ; but how he looked, how he was
dressed, how tall he was, whether he was
black, brown, or white, she knew no more
than whither the rest of these caves tended.
She said—

'How long do you think I have been
down here?'

'I should say half an hour,' he answered.

'You mean ten minutes,' she cried.

'Well, time lengthens itself whilst we
stop in this place,' he exclaimed.   'If we
have missed the avenue leading to the exit,
we   may   go   hunting   endlessly   through
corridors for it.'

'No,' she exclaimed passionately.   'If I
can see the daylight in the end, I shall know
where I am.'

They walked, and they continued to walk.
Ada's heart turned cold with horror.   She
had no true conception of the ramifications
of these remarkable caves, and did not know

but that there might be wells and desperate
pits many feet deep sunk in some of the
windings. They all, no doubt, had their
hatchways or exits, long since buried under
the sands of time. Evidently it was a great
company of smugglers who had fashioned
this Devil's Walk.

'Where are we going?' said the man,
stopping; and Ada Conway stopped.

'I sha'n't know until I see the light in
the passage where I met you.'

'The mischief is,' cried the man, 'that
we may be walking yoked round and round
endlessly, without ever coming to either
light. Good God, what a horrible issue to
this adventure! Nobody ever visits this
place, I suppose?'

'Only you,' said she; 'and it's my
business to save you.'

'How sorry I am that you should be here
I can't say, yet it is natural to want to get
out.'

'But it seems so mad to come into this
smuggler's hole with a dream of booty, with
no further provision than a candle; and it is
wonderful that you should not know by that

same light that you had been entombed, and spent a whole night underground !'

' Time flies and time loiters under wild conditions. I can tell you that, for I'm a sailor.'

' Are you ?' she ejaculated. ' What rating ?'

' I lately commanded a merchantman. I have lain awake all night sick in hospital, and have heard the quarters and halves strike with the rapidity of chimes. I could not have sworn that three hours have passed. I shall *look* the time, I suspect, when I get out. I am beginning to feel a bit weary of this blackness, and long for that one round of light that offered me a leap as an escape.'

As he spoke these words they made a step, and lo ! on their left, at the extremity of the passage, glowed, within fifty feet, the cheery star of day.

' Hurrah !' shouted the man.

The girl, in a single sob, unheard by her companion, expressed her pent-up feelings.

' Yes, there's the port-hole right enough,' said the man. ' Now you know the way.'

' Come along straight,' she said.

She led him as before, and touching the wall, made a true course for the opening. But as she advanced she grew very uneasy on observing that no light fell through the hatch-hole, and that the short flight of steps was not visible in any definition of colour. Her companion, stumbling slowly alongside of her, presently noticed this.

'How did you get in?' said he.

'By a trap which I left open.'

'It isn't night again, I hope,' said he, with a ghastly laugh.

'I see no light,' she answered, 'and this is the corridor of the entrance. Oh, my God! I fear some meddlesome wretch, whilst I've been talking to you, instead of hastening above, has shut us down.'

'So that we can't get out?'

'Not from within.'

'Well,' said he, after a pause, and with a tone of courage in his voice, 'what we've got to do is to go to that light-hole yonder and wait for something to pass, and make our case known. Somebody is sure to pass.'

'Let me see if I can feel the steps with my foot,' said the girl. 'But hold on to me.'

He had brought out a large metal tinder-box—but empty ; and in his fit of distraction let it fall. She shrieked as if she had been stung. The nerves of even stout-hearted girls soon yield to blackness, to the association of strange invisible men, and to the probability of a frightful fate. He laughed to encourage her, said what the thing was, and groped and picked it up. She took him to the steps, felt with her foot, and said, 'Feel for yourself. The trap-door is immediately overhead.'

'Well, if we mean to preserve our lives,' said the man—'and God knows how sorry I am that you should be here sharing my imbecile fate—we must walk to that round hole yonder, and keep a smart look-out on the sands below. But I'll try first if this stone can be lifted by shoving.'

He left her and got upon the short set of steps, and strained with his hands. He could not bring his shoulder to bear. In vain. He toiled and groaned. He came down, and feeling for her, said, 'No ; the sight-seers have made it easy from above ; but it is not easy to thrust up from under, and if I were twenty men I could not do it with my hands in that narrow circumference.'

'Let's walk to that hole,' said the girl, hooking him. 'It is our only chance.'

'Another sight-seer may descend,' said he.

'Few dream of booty in this age,' she answered. 'It is pretty well known,' she continued, 'that all are dry bones here.'

They gained the orifice. It framed a noble picture of Channel ocean afternoon. The seas ridged in glittering ranks, smoke burst from their curtseying heads, and they raced in groans upon the hidden beach beneath, whitening out back to half a mile of foam. Ships were in sight, blowing upwards, blowing downwards, rendered somewhat prismatic in the airy lens of that smuggler's window. The tide was making fast, and they could see nothing but white water.

'Look at that,' cried the man, pointing down.

The shuddering girl drew a foot or two closer, and peered below. 'There is no escape !' she exclaimed.

Now they looked at each other. The

girl has been described. The man was the
sailorly-looking fellow you would expect to
see in him, after his confession of his calling.
The light shone very well here, and sank
for a distance of twenty or thirty feet into
the gloom, then went out in utter sudden-
ness into black blankness. Miss Conway
saw standing beside her a man of about
thirty years of age. He was dressed in the
style of the day when Peace had newly
lighted on the land, when the billows of our
home waters were no longer vexed by the
keels of contending cruisers, nor by their
thunder. He was decidedly handsome.
Hair cut short behind. He had lost his
hat, and she could see that his hair in front
was bushy and plentiful, coming over the
forehead in the 'fine' style of that age. He
had very striking features, but they looked
ashen and sunken now. He bowed to the
young lady when their gaze met, and said,
raising his hand—

'You perceive I have lost my hat.'

'We will not seek it,' she exclaimed.

He was dressed in a dark green cloth coat,
a coloured waistcoat and metal buttons. He

was covered with dust, had scratched himself
on the hands and face, and could not have
looked in a more sorry plight had he been
newly enlarged after a week's imprisonment
in the great Pyramid.

'Do no persons but you ever walk along
these sands when they are bare?' said the man.

'At long intervals,' said she, finding some
faint reassurance in his presence and in the
light. 'A boatman or a stranger in the
place might stroll as far as this from the
town. The tide is ugly, and it makes fast.'

'At that rate we are entombed, and must
die in the full sight of life,' cried the man,
leaning against the wall, and folding his arms
with a scowl. 'It is bad enough that I
should be here, cursed idiot that I am! But
that I should have drawn you into a living
grave!'

'I desire you will act as a man,' she interrupted passionately. 'We must husband our
strength and preserve our voices. In to-day
or in to-morrow'—but her tones failed her
as she spoke—'a man may pass within
reach of our voice, and learning who I am,
deliver us.'

He gazed at her with a sudden admiration. She certainly made a noble heroic figure as she stood viewing him in that strange tunnel-like light, bright on the left, in gloom on the right. Her eyes sparkled. She looked down the corridor where the steps lay, then sat down, placing her back against the wall. It was clear that an under-dread possessed her, but not so as to master her. The thought of being locked down with a strange man in a lonely cavern for an afternoon and night—and for how much longer, who could tell ?—was horrible ; it kept her soul shuddering, so to speak. But the man's own consternation was too excessive to take notice of anything but this : that he was entombed in a smugglers' cave where, as things stood, there was every chance of their leaving their bones. He squatted in a most disconsolate posture opposite to her, and they both had the light on them.

' This,' said the man, meaning the light, ' is worth something, anyhow.'

' Continual darkness is frightful,' she answered ; ' it drives men mad.'

' Who the deuce could figure that those

sands would be covered at flood?' he cried. 'What an enormous waste they offer when the water is low!'

'You must have slept, otherwise you would surely know that you had already spent a night in this place.'

'When I found I couldn't get out,' he answered, 'I took to wandering in the darkness, and lost the light, and losing that, lost this corridor. I turned and plied and groped, and then my candle being burnt out, I sat down as I now sit, and I have no doubt I slept. I awoke, and began to grope my way along again, and after a long time my hands brought me to some entrance just down yonder, clear into the view of this orifice.'

'Was it daylight?' she asked.

'Bright.'

'When you get out,' said she, smiling faintly, 'you will have had enough of the Devil's Walk.'

'I shall thank God for my escape, madam,' cried he, with real fervour, 'if it is only for your preservation. May I venture to ask the name of the good and heroic lady who has

come at the risk of her life to release a man
from a living tomb ?'

'My name is Ada Conway,' she answered.
He stood up and made her a low bow.

'My father is Commander Conway, late
of the Royal Navy—what he will think—
what he will fear—the fruitless searches he
will be making—I am his only child—he
will suppose I have been overtaken by the
tide and drowned. Yet they should still be
looking for me there,' she exclaimed, gazing
out to sea.

'No, madam, they wouldn't creep in the
surf,' said he; 'they'd watch for the breakers
to strand you. Permit me to introduce
myself. I am Captain Jackman, late of the
ship *Lovelace*, which arrived home a week or
two ago. I left her, and having heard much
of these parts, thought I would make a cruise
to your neighbourhood, and a pretty cruise it
has been.'

'Are you an American ?' she asked.

'No. I am supposed to descend from a
good old English family.'

'You have had no food since yesterday ?'

'Not a pinch of biscuit.'

'Well, God must help us out.   He must help us out, for it is too, *too* awful,' she cried, burying her face.

'If people don't pass to-day, they will come along to-morrow,' said Captain Jackman ; 'and I have got the voice of a lion.' Saying which, he stood up and sent ' Ship ahoy !   For God's sake, help us,' slinging in ringing echoes across the troubled breast of the sea.

'Ay !' she exclaimed ; 'but think what must pass between now and to-morrow.' She looked at her watch.   'Do you know the time ?' she inquired.

'By the light in the west, I should say it is not far from six,' he answered.

'It is six,' she said, replacing her watch, 'and we have the night before us.'

'It must be borne,' said the man, with a note of sulky sympathy, clasping his knees, and fixing his eyes upon the sea.

CHAPTER II.

IT was about two o'clock in the morning, as they came afterwards to know, when Ada Conway sprang, with a violent ringing shriek, to her feet. She had been sitting close to the sphere in the cliff. Opposite to her squatted the man, apparently in slumber. The disc framed a scene of midnight heavens full of palpitating stars, and slowly moving snow-white clouds sailing northwards, and a corner of moon like a silver spear-head nestling in and visibly departing from the top arch of the orifice.

The girl shrieked, and the man also sprang to his feet.

' We are saved !' he shouted.

He caught her by the hand, and began to run. In the direction of the steps there was glowing a considerable glare of torchlight, amidst which the forms of several figures were clearly distinguishable, and whilst the pair ran, a voice, loud as a trumpet, came in echoes down through the hollow vault.

' Is Miss Ada Conway below here ?'

' Yes,' screamed the girl.

' God Almighty !   Come to your father ! What are you doing in these vaults ?'   And the figure that was speaking started on perceiving, by the strong torchlight, that the girl approached with a male companion.

The commander was a little square man of the ' Boarders away !' type, equal, in his heyday, when in charge of a boat and crew, to a French or Spanish gunboat.   He had been one of the most gallant officers in the service, and had quitted it as commander on an income of his own.

Ada, recognising him by the light, threw herself upon his breast in a wild storm of weeping.   She sobbed ; the commander stood silent, surveying the handsome bareheaded stranger, who was very visible in the flashes the torch-bearers waved about him. Then collecting herself with a sudden sense of rapture at the thought that she was safe, and with her father, she lifted her head, and holding her father's arm, exclaimed—

'Father, this is Captain Jackman. I was passing along the sands yesterday morning——'

'So! *Yesterday* morning! *How* many yesterday mornings do you mean ?' groaned the commander.

'When,' continued the girl, 'I heard this gentleman crying for help out through that hole there. I came on to the green and got between the rails, and managed to lift the stone and descended. We forgot ourselves in talk ; we lost ourselves in deviating from right to left. When we came to this place it was in total blackness ; the stone was on, and we were entombed.'

'Let's get on deck,' said Commander Conway.

They passed up through the trap, five of them, lighting the land for a mile around. How gloriously sweet and fresh and boundless was the night ! The piece of silver moon shone over the sea and shed a little light upon the earth. The stars sparkled,

3

and the white clouds floated with a majest y
that befitted their domain.   Ada passed her
hand through her father's arm on rising out
of the earth, and exclaimed—

'Who could have put the hatch down
upon me, father ?   There was no man in
sight when I went to let Captain Jackman
out.'

'He was that fellow Goldsmith,' answered
the commander.   'He is one of the torch-
bearers.   He instantly came to apprise me,
on recollecting.   He said he fell asleep after
walking from Spenpoor, just past a brow
of land where you couldn't see him.   No
sooner had you gone down than he must
have got up, and finding the cover off, put
it on, according to the custom of these
rogues.'

'The wretch,' cried the girl, turning and
straining her eyes at the three men in their
rear.   'Couldn't you have guessed, you
savage, by sign of that stone being off,' she
shouted at Goldsmith, 'that there must be
people in the caves below ?'

'I vow to Peter, then,' cried Goldsmith,
waving his torch furiously so that the figures

of the people came and went in a cannibal
dance of glow, ' that I thought it was some
wicked trick of a boy, or that it had been
forgotten, and so I put it on again. God
forgive me.'

' Who are you ?' said Captain Jackman,
addressing the other torch-bearer.

' My name is Herman, and I am a poor
boatman,' answered the man. ' I've got
nothing to do with this job.'

' Here,' said the captain, in the brisk tone
of the sea ; and he slipped a sovereign into
his hand. ' Here, you Goldsmith,' and he
also slipped a sovereign into the hand of the
excited torch-bearer. ' See here,' said he,
' you pinned this lady down, and you might
have killed us both. You might for sixpence, some ten years hence, have gone
below and started back at beholding two
skeletons lying athwart the entrance corridor.
But you did not mean it. You were quick
in your turn when reflection came to our
service. So take this.'

The man was profound in his bows and
brow-knuckling by the faint light of the
moon. The conversation had been listened

to in silence by the commander and his daughter.

'You've lost your 'at, sir. Shall I fetch it for yer ?' said Goldsmith.

'I wouldn't send a wolf into that Devil's Walk,' answered Captain Jackman, with a dull laugh.

'We'll find your 'at, sir,' said the two men, and they plunged away back towards the broken fence and the hole in the earth.

'I wonder,' exclaimed Captain Jackman, coming abreast of Commander Conway, 'if my little hotel will be open at this hour ?' and he gazed down at the short square man who trotted between him and his daughter, whose head towered above her father's.

'No need to talk of hotels, sir. Happy to put you up, I'm sure, after your desperate experiences. My house is close by, and, sir,' he said, turning, and extending his hand and clasping that of Captain Jackman, 'I thank you, from the heart of a father, for your courtesy during these long hours to my daughter.'

Captain Jackman shook the old gentleman

by the hand and bowed, but made no reply; and they resumed their walk.

All their talk, till they arrived at the commander's cottage, was about this singular adventure under earth. Captain Jackman freely owned this—

' I wouldn't take a guide, for my hopes denied me one; frankly and truthfully, commander, I had been told that some smugglers' booty lay in a branch tunnel of this hiding-place, and my intention was to look at it, and afterwards to take measures to secure it by passing it through the window.'

The commander's laugh had the sepulchral note of the Devil's Walk.

' We were famous smugglers in our time, sir,' said he; ' we did not leave our run goods, earned at the very risk of our lives, to be fetched and enjoyed by strangers to the gang.'

' Who told you of a treasure lurking in an English cliff ?' asked Miss Conway.

' The master of a brigantine,' answered the captain, ' who knew your little creek or port well, and the whole of the smugglers who had thronged it, before the lawless lot discovered their diggings were of no use to them, and departed.'

'That's not so long ago either,' said the commander. 'It's not above four years since that, from these cliffs, I witnessed one of the most desperate actions I ever saw between a large smuggler cutter and a Government schooner. They made a running fight, then came to a stand with wrecked canvas and blazing guns. They fought with extravagant courage, sir; then the smuggler, with his scuppers running crimson, threw his sweeps over, and by heaven the schooner remained silent and active only in making good the mischief done her.'

'It is abominably hard,' said Ada, 'to kill men for smuggling. I like the price of smuggled tea.'

'And what tobacco, sir, tastes like the run stuff?' said the captain.

'Here's my home,' said the commander.

He pushed open a front garden-gate. The house lay in blackness, save that in one corner a square of window was dimly illuminated. No lights were visible beyond in the neighbourhood of the town. It was three o'clock in the morning, growing into four, and the vast dome of midnight fast and faster flashed with stars as the morning grew. The horizon vanished in blackness thrilling with the white of charging seas.

'Captain Jackman is ready to die of hunger, father, and of thirst also,' said Miss Conway, as the party of three stepped along the walk.

'He shall be fed,' said the commander. 'You'll be perished, Ada, I don't doubt.'

He put a key into his door, opened it, and they entered.

An elderly woman in a dressing-gown, her hair curiously curled, her figure immensely stout, was descending the staircase, holding high a candle as they entered. She seemed to fall off the stairs, shrieking—

'I heard your voices. Oh, Miss Ada, where have you been hiding yourself?'

'Thanks, Mrs. Dove, I am safe, and am fortunate in having saved the life of another,' said Miss Conway, scarcely enduring the old housekeeper's embrace, and motioning towards Captain Jackman, to whom the stout old woman bowed.

Mrs. Dove had been twenty-two years in Commander Conway's family; had nursed Ada until she was too old to require a nurse; had nursed Mrs. Conway through a long, most distressing and fatal illness; and was now, in her somewhat advanced middle age, appointed by the commander, in gratitude for services rendered, to the honourable post of chief mate of his little craft.

'We want something to eat, Mrs. Dove,' said Ada. 'Is the servant up?'

'No, miss. I let her lie. I could not know you were coming.'

She pulled a small bell which rang upstairs, and they all went into the little room that was lighted by a candle. The commander lighted four or five more candles, and this made light to see by.

'No,' said Ada. 'I'll not go upstairs until I go to bed, and then I'll sleep for a week. I am not fearfully tunnel-soiled, I hope.' And she stood up and turned herself about, to the admiration of Captain Jackman.

It was a comfortable room that sparkled

out to those slender beams of candle. The commander had had a little money with his wife, and had put good furniture into his home. Some maritime pictures of stirring excellence hung upon his walls. A great silver plate blazed at the back of the sideboard : the silver had been left out in the excitement of that night. Captain Jackman looked around him.

' How far is it from here to the " Faithful Heart " ?' said he.

' You'll measure it easily in half an hour,' answered the commander, whilst Mrs. Dove went out to prepare a meal for them. ' But why not sleep here? You may find it hard to get into your inn.'

The captain bowed.

' I fear,' said he, addressing Ada, ' that I have sufficiently embarrassed you. Since one o'clock yesterday morning in a dark pit, with a shadowy stranger, and with a prospect of a dreadful death confronting you ! Miss Conway,' he said, bowing to her with shining eyes, ' you are the bravest young lady I have ever read or heard of, and you deserve a great heroic admiral for a husband.'

This was a queer compliment; she laughed, nevertheless, in clear enjoyment of his speech: indeed, she got few speeches of any sort from good-looking men, from men of any kind. This even the commander secretly admitted to himself was a peculiarly handsome man who had complimented her.

A maid-servant, owl-like with wonder and sleep, stumbled in with a tray of beef and bread, and beer, and other matters. Mrs. Dove followed. She placed the candles and the chairs, and threatened to wait. The commander told her to go to bed and take the girl with her. He then took the head of the table, and carved liberal trenchers for the famished pair.

'This is good beer,' said the captain, putting his mug down with a deep sigh.

'We are dull, but what we have is good. Our views are magnificent, and although Ada would like to live in London and dwell within musket-shot of St. James's Palace, I am satisfied, and therefore happy.' He added suddenly, 'Jackman! The name recurs to me. I think I saw a paragraph in a little sheet that makes its way here-abouts, stating that a Captain Jackman of the ship *Lovelace* had been knocked down in London, and robbed of fifteen hundred pounds.'

' I am that man, sir,' said the captain, without any emotion in his face.

' Was the money recovered ?' said the commander.

' Not a dollar.'

' Have you any suspicions as to the thief ?' inquired Miss Conway.

' I believe he is a dirty little forecastle hand, who got scent that I was carrying the money ashore, and followed me,' answered Captain Jackman. ' I saw such a figure disappear as it threw my bag down an area.'

' Fifteen hundred pounds is a considerable slice for a merchant vessel to lose in these times, sir,' said the commander.

' And a merchant vessel is a considerable slice for a master to lose at all times, sir,' answered Captain Jackman.

' Have they dismissed you ?' inquired Ada.

' Yes,' said the captain with a careless laugh, ' and so I came down here to enjoy myself by getting locked down in a cave, and making for one of the ugliest of deaths. How can I thank you—how can I thank you, madam ?' he said, languishing towards Ada.

Just then a single knock fell upon the hall door, and the commander returned with Captain Jackman's round hat.

'Thanks for all things,' he exclaimed, as he took it.

'I wonder, sir,' remarked the commander, 'that you should have thought proper to venture your life in an underground cutting with one candle only.'

'It was a tall candle,' answered the captain ; 'and I did not think that I was going below to be locked down.'

'True !' exclaimed old Conway.

Captain Jackman, in these few moments of pause in the talk, seemed to make an askant study of the commander, who sat opposite. The light was poor for facial revelations. He distinguished a rather stern expression, brows heavily thatched with white hair, a nearly bald head, with the white hair cut short about the ears. He was disproportionately square, and sat a massive figure. The captain's scrutiny was brief. He turned his eyes upon the young lady, whose eyes met his; then he looked at the clock.

'I am the cause of keeping you out of bed,' he said, rising. 'Will you permit me to retire?'

'Show the captain his room, Ada,' said the commander.

The girl lighted a rush-light that was upon the hall table, and led the way upstairs, and the commander followed, calmly receiving the impassioned shake of the hand Captain Jackman bestowed upon him.

That morning at ten o'clock Captain Jackman awoke, and found himself in a snug little bedroom of white dimity, trembling with brilliance that streamed upon the blinds from the sea. As he got out of bed, he heard a woman singing low and clear. He raised the blinds, and beheld a prospect that assuredly justified Commander Conway's choice of residence. No loftiest mast-head yields you a grander scene. It was painted here and there with a ship, and was coloured blue and white, and the heavens bent blue to the edge of it; but a number of clouds of delicate shape, and charged with a dark softness of rain, were rolling up from the south-west.

'This is a home to suit me,' thought the captain, and, hearing the girl singing either next door or downstairs, he fell a-musing.

The maidservant, answering his bell, brought him the commander's razor and some hot water, and in twenty minutes he was downstairs. The house door was open, and the commander walked up and down his lawn, smoking a pipe of Dutch pattern. He showed himself by daylight as a man of strong features, heavily bronzed, as by years of travel. His eyes were a keen blue, and deep set, and his mouth a curl, the under lip slightly protruding.

'Good-morning, sir !' he exclaimed to the captain. 'I hope you slept well.'

The usual civilities were exchanged.

'Breakfast will be ready when my daughter is pleased to appear. She is risen,' said the commander.

'I have been listening to her charming voice. Is she your only child, sir ?'

'I lost a promising young son in the navy eight years ago,' answered the commander.

'I served as midshipman in the navy,' exclaimed Captain Jackman.

'Oh!' said the commander, with sudden interest. 'What ship and captain, sir?'

'The *Parkhurst*; Captain Trottman.'

'I knew them both. A fine frigate, and a stout seaman. Why didn't you stick to the service?'

'Why, the life of the mercantile flag was free and easy; it offered more money; it provided plenty of voyages and chances. I never particularly coveted the glory that was to be got in the navy. I should want my flag first.'

'That sort of glory is a slow sunrise with us, sir,' said the commander.

'Then, again, I was to a certain degree independent,' continued Captain Jackman, talking in a careless, confidential way. 'My father had left me an annuity—not, indeed, enough to roll on wheels with—that and a small, handsome brig under two hundred tons, now lying in the East India Dock. I have often been tempted to sell her. Now that my kindly owners have given me my quietus through no fault of my own, I have a very great mind to fit her out——'

'And go for a cruise on the Account,' interrupted the clear voice of a girl.

And Captain Jackman, turning, clasped the extended hand of Miss Conway.

Her garb was simple and charming. The hat she held was a kind of helmet, with a wreath and a tuft of feathers. She stood in the pride of her fine but simple apparel.

'Breakfast should be ready,' said the commander.

He led the way into the house. Captain Jackman and Miss Conway followed, chatting with life and spirit over the wonderful incident of yesterday. How could such a heart-shaking sensation be exhausted! The commander had furnished a savoury breakfast of large fried soles and delicate fried whiting, and bacon and eggs. They seated themselves; and when the captain had concluded his apologies for detaining the commander, he turned to Miss Conway, and said—

'You have read books which deal with pirates ?'

'Yes. Papa will tell you that I was ever a lover of the pirate. I mean the real thing, not the Byronic dandy with his bright costume and four or five houris and lovely homes on coral strands. I love the rough brute with a slash across his brow—the man who has lost a piece of his nose, who, perhaps, has captured a Spanish galleon whilst skipper of a vessel of twenty or thirty tons.'

'It has been done,' said the commander. 'If there's a scoundrel this side the moon, it's the pirate. All the woods of Scotland could not furnish gibbets enough for him. Give the piccaroon the stem, you know. That's the cry through the service, sir. We'd show mercy to anything else.'

'In spite of my father's objections to pirates, Captain Jackman,' said Ada Conway, leaning back in her chair, and beginning to laugh, and showing a fine set of white and even teeth, 'if I had your ship, I would equip her as a privateer, and sail away as a

4

sea-robber.   What splendid luck should *always* attend such enterprises, seeing that your quarry is the clumsy, unprepared, easily-frightened merchantman ! whilst you —a single broadside might settle the matter, and win you enough treasure to fill you a large cave with.'

Captain Jackman, laughing lightly and gazing with admiration at the young lady, tapped applause of her sentiments with his knife upon the table.

' I would advise you to stick to the honourable red flag,' said the commander.

' Freights are always ruling low, as they call it,' answered the captain, ' and a man wants an office and a book-keeper ; and there are expenses ashore going on,' said he, addressing the commander, but with occasional side looks at Ada.   ' But, depend on't, any scheme I may form shall provide for my neck.'

' I cannot, I will say, consider the revenue worth the loss of a drop of blood, were it not for the officials of it,' said the commander, who was making a great breakfast off fried sole.

' How are your blockaders coming forward, sir ?' inquired the captain.

'They are very sparsely settled at present, and they are not coming forward. I doubt if there's half-a-dozen preventives betwixt this and St. Ives. It must grow into a considerable force if it is to protect the revenue. They keep their few best men about Folkestone and Ramsgate; and *there* the fighting is mostly going on. Calais is near; so is Dunkirk. The Goodwins are convenient for dodging.'

'What could have made them construct such caves as Miss Conway and I were locked up in ?' asked the captain.

'They probably had an idea. In the middle of it they found that it would not work out, so they dropped it with the dexterity of men accustomed to rapidity of thought and action.'

' I believe there are similar caves some leagues round the coast—Cornwall way— perhaps in Cornwall,' said the captain.

The girl, looking at him a little expressively, said, ' You had better take two candles with you next time.'

He smiled and bowed, whilst she was all geniality and kindness, in arch humour of fair face of gipsy cast.

'I do not believe, madam,' said he, 'that I shall disturb the silence of another smuggler's cell.'

'Booty or no booty?'

'Don't mislead the gentleman, Ada,' exclaimed her father. 'There is no booty. I would not give the value of this button,' said he, fingering one of his coat-buttons, 'for the whole of the booty that you shall find deliberately left, never more to be fetched by these free-traders.'

'I had hoped,' said Ada, whose eyes shone over her mounted colour, 'that you were going to submit a romantic project; I am very romantic myself. I could die for a lovely young man.'

The commander grinned.

'If he was worth dying for. Must he be lovely?' said Captain Jackman, pushing his chair from the table and nursing his knee, and regarding her with obstinate pleasure, for he not only found her a handsome woman; she had saved his life at the risk of her own.

'I had thought,' continued the girl, 'from the interest you take in these caves, and by your accent, which is slightly American——'

'Ho!' cried the captain, 'that's news to me.'

'That you were going to fit out your brig with some romantic reference to these holes in the rocks. Strange ideas enter one's head.'

'They do indeed, madam.'

They rose from the table. The captain, turning to the commander, said, putting all the graceful bows and courtesy of that age into his demeanour—

'Will you, commander, and Miss Conway, give me the pleasure, the real pleasure— of your company at dinner at the " Faithful Heart "? Say six o'clock.'

The commander seemed to pause. The girl's eyes burnt upon him. He began a little awkwardly—

'As strangers, sir, we really have no claim.'

'Do not speak of me as a stranger, I beg,' said the captain.

The commander looked at his daughter, saw a quarrel in her fine eyes, sulkiness running into days, much discomfort to an elderly widower living with an only child, and so he whipped out—

'Be it so, captain. We will be with you at six o'clock.'

Shortly after this, Captain Jackman left the pretty little house, having stood a few minutes by Miss Conway's side, greatly admiring the spacious view from the lawn. The commander walked to the side of his daughter, who remained on the lawn, watching the departing figure of Captain Jackman.

'What do you think of him, father?' said she, laying her hand upon his square shoulder.

'Think! He is no introduction of yours that we should *think*,' cried the little seaman.

'You know him through me, and cannot but have thoughts about him, good or bad,' she exclaimed, with an irritable toss of her head, dropping her hand.

'Well, betwixt you and me,' said the commander, turning to take a view of his house, 'I don't like him.'

' Oh, I knew it would be so !' she exclaimed. ' He is much too handsome. Had I appeared in the company of an old man of sixty, with a brown wig down his back, and a yellow nose down his face, you would have found him a welcome presence.'

The commander did not readily lose his temper. ' I do not like this man because I do not like his manner of losing fifteen hundred pounds—the property of others. It is strange. It is peculiar. It is memorable. And I recollected it, as you may have observed, when we were seated.'

' Was it good taste ?' said the girl, slightly sneering.

' Oh, we don't live in these parts to cultivate what you call taste ! We speak the truth—or should.'

' What do you want to imply, father ?'

The commander looked at the ocean and grinned.

' You mean to say,' continued the girl, ' that Captain Jackman knocked himself down and robbed his owners of fifteen hundred pounds ?'

'They do not charge him with it; why should I, whatever I may think?'   And humming a popular song of that day, the commander turned on his heel and went into his house.

His daughter remained on the lawn— looking at the sea, do you think?   No; but at the fast disappearing figure of Captain Jackman, whom, on her own confession, she thought a handsome man.   A handsome man was of more interest and rarity than a sea view, which she had gazed at hundreds of times o'er and o'er.   The race of the sea flashed in vain; its heavy guns of breakers thundered at deaf ears; that fine frigate abreast, with canvas white as driven snow so leaning as to expose a portion of her bright copper, the long wake bubbling and rushing, swept through the deep before blind eyes.   No beauty of cloud, of liquid, or land recess could arrest her; she saw but a figure, and when it vanished, she re-entered the house with a very thoughtful face.

Captain Jackman walked straight into the little town.   A little town it was, with one good, and two or three middling streets.   It had a row of houses called the Lawn, and most of the important people of the town lived there. Captain Jackman went straight to the 'Faithful Heart,' and entered the darkling bar that had a brightness of reflected oak, and of highly polished pewter, and said to the woman who sat sewing behind—

'You see I have returned, Mrs. Davis !'

'God bless me ! Yes,' cried the little woman, starting from her chair, dropping her work, and staring at him. 'We all gave you up for drowned.'

'I was in direr plight—I was entombed.'

Asking for a glass of brandy, he told her the story, whilst the landlord came in from the backyard to listen. He then went upstairs to his bedroom. He looked at himself in the glass, and seemed satisfied. The scars of the night of darkness had worn off, the tunnel stains had vanished. He took a considerable sum of money in gold out of his portmanteau or valise, and went downstairs. He called to Mrs. Davis.

'A word with you in your front parlour, madam.'

She rose, curtseyed, and conducted him to a front room of a fair size.

'This will do,' said Captain Jackman. 'Here's quite room enough. I want to give a dinner to two friends at six o'clock to-night. Can you manage it for me?'

'You shall have the best that is to be had, sir; and I may truly say that my cooking is known far and wide.'

'The guests are Commander Conway and his daughter. Do you know them?'

'By sight and name, sir. They are a little——' And here, not choosing to abase herself, she curtseyed.

Why should worthy Mrs. Davis have told the handsome gentleman that Miss Conway would no more have regarded her than the mould she trod on?

'I will make out a list of dishes now,' said the captain.

Mrs. Davis fetched a pencil and slate, and Captain Jackman, in the time that the well-known poet, Smithson, takes to turn out a sonnet, safe in the applause of fifty other Smithsons, had made out a really handsome dinner for those days of plain dishes. He then left the inn, and walked slowly up the High Street, looking into the shops on either hand, until he came to a jeweller's shop, at which he made a stand.

After inspecting the furnished window, he entered, and said to a bald-headed man behind the counter—

'This is a little place for a big order.'

'I hope not, sir. There may be larger shops, but there are not a better class of goods.'

'I want the very best,' said Captain Jackman, looking darkly at the bald head. 'Show me the best bracelets in your possession.'

'At what price?' stammered the old fool.

'I said the best,' thundered Captain Jackman, 'and I want one without delay.'

The man with the bald head produced a number of bracelets. They were not very good. He knew it, and did not make much of them. The captain pish'd and tossed them, and was going, when the bald-headed man cried out suddenly, as to an inspiration—

'I beg your pardon, sir. Six months

ago, a family in this neighbourhood failed, and amongst the stuff sold was their jewellery. Some of it came into my hands. I can let you have the most magnificent bracelet you ever saw, providing that you don't care that it is second-hand, and I will give you a guarantee that I will return the money should the lady find out that it was ever worn.'

' Right,' said the captain.

The man disappeared, and the captain stood in the shop door looking at the town ; then returned on the jeweller re-entering. The man, with a proud eye, placed on the counter a very beautiful bracelet, of old pattern, sparkling with diamonds and precious stones, massive, and wrought into some device of serpent.

' London shall not beat this, sir,' said the shopkeeper.

' This suits me,' answered Captain Jack-man. ' How much ?'

The shopkeeper had clearly just made up his mind.

' It is a second-hand article, sir. I'll not charge you more than forty-five guineas.'

The captain carefully examined the thing. He admired it hugely; it was probably a hundred years old, and was, perhaps, cheap at a hundred guineas. It was a beautiful gift for a beautiful woman, and the captain, putting it down, pulled out a handful of gold. The bald-headed jeweller stared at the sight of so much money. He was to stare at another handful before forty-five guineas could be told.

'Pack it,' said Captain Jackman, in the abrupt commanding manner of the sea; 'and give me a pen and ink and paper, that I may send a letter with it.'

The jeweller cleared a little table for him, and set a chair at it, and the captain began to write. It was a fine, dashing hand, a gentleman's hand.

'I have respectfully to entreat Miss Conway's acceptance of the accompanying trifling memorial of an incident which must have turned out a terrible tragedy to me, but for her noble bravery. So poor a jewel cannot possibly express the sensations which accompany it.

'WALTER JACKMAN.'

By the time this letter was written, the jeweller had packed the bracelet.

'Address it,' said the captain, and he gave the address. This done, he exclaimed, 'Have you got a messenger you can trust ?'

'I have my son, sir.'

The son was working upstairs. In a few minutes he was on his way to the home of the Conways, with the beautiful gift and letter in his pocket, whilst Captain Jackman, bestowing a farewell nod on the jeweller, stepped forth to take a view of the town, and to see what the little harbour was like.

CHAPTER III.

THE DINNER.

Captain Jackman walked down the steep street watched by the jeweller and a hairdresser who had stepped from opposite when the captain marched off.

'A few of him would open these cliffs and let in more houses and people. God bless me! I never thought to sell it, and *yet* he's got a bargain.'

'What's the article?' inquired the hairdresser.

'A bracelet. It's cost him forty-five guineas. I believe he'd have given a hundred for it.'

'What is he, do you think?'

'A sailor, I should say.'

'Did he pay cash?'

'Bright cash.' And the jeweller, half-closing one eye, pulled out a handful of glittering sovereigns, at which the hair-dresser gazed with admiration.

'Perhaps he's the gent that got himself lost in the Devil's Walk,' said the hair-dresser.

The jeweller smote his thigh and cried, 'That's it! And the bracelet's gone to Miss Conway.'

Captain Jackman disappeared from their gaze. He turned the corner of the long gap, which was scarcely made a street of by the row of houses on top, and found on the right a short wooden wharf about whose piles the seas were toiling. A number of fine fishing-boats lay off this wharf, and rode the rolling comber with perfect grace to their anchors. Westward, beyond this wharf, was a sort of natural harbour; but it was evident that the place was only used by the men for convenience, and that they landed their catches in other harbours.

'Well, what's doing here?' said Captain Jackman to a tall, powerfully built seaman in the rough dress, heavy boots, belt, and hanging cap of those times.

'There we are,' said the man, pointing to the smacks rolling broadside on to the wharf.

'But do you fish in this part?' said the captain.

The strong man, with a face put together in pieces like masses of putty, answered—

'We fish where we think there is anything to be caught.'

'What's the smuggler doing down here now?'

'Oh, they're all gone away to the east-'ard!' answered the man, with a note of indifference.

'But they thought well of this place once upon a time. Men must live to learn that they're fools. Who would sail a hundred and fifty miles to run a cargo when he may set it ashore on this coast with only the danger of a third of the distance? Were you ever at sea as a sailor?' said the captain.

The man smiled, and showed his immense yellow teeth, and, pulling off his cap, combed down his grisly hair.

'I've served at sea on blue water thirty years. I've come to this because I can earn more money by it. I've served in men-o'-war and merchantmen, and was second mate of the West Indiaman *Sirius*.'

'What's your name ?' said the captain.

'Bill Hoey,' answered the man.

'Where do you live ?'

The man gave his address, which Captain Jackman entered, along with the name, in a pocket-book.

'Have you got any family ?' said the captain.

'An old mother turned of ninety. I buried my sunshine twenty year ago.'

'How would you like to take a voyage with me in a fine brig ?'

'On what errand ?'

'Simply a voyage of discovery. We would discourse that matter on board, when all hands were assembled.'

'How would you rate me ?'

'Can you take the altitude of the sun ?'

'Yes, sir.'

'You shall be my chief mate. I like your looks.'

The man grinned and said, 'How about the money, sir ?'

' I am my own owner. There will be no difficulty about wages. Here's my name and address.'

He scribbled them on a fly-leaf of his note-book, tore the leaf out, and the man, after reading it, put it into his breast.

' If you know of other likely lads who have a fancy for a brisk and merry voyage from London town to the Land of Romance, and who are willing to count their pay in sovereigns instead of shillings, I shall feel obliged to you,' said the captain.

Bill Hoey touched his cap. He was beginning to regard this gentleman with admiration.

The captain stood bending his brows in a searching glance along the ten or dozen men who were hanging about the wooden wharf, leaning against the timber heads smoking and talking in growling notes ; then with a sharp ' Good day,' he whipped round and walked up the gap.

When he arrived on top of the cliffs, he turned to his left and walked a couple of miles along the edge, pausing where a curve gave him a view of the coast. He sought also with keen eyes inland. It was clear from his looks, after he had turned on his heel and struck for the town, that this place, or its vicinity, was not to his taste. He pulled out his pipe and lighted it; but the brave wind, gushing in a blue fountain over the edge of the cliff, made but a short smoke of it for him.

He amused himself in various ways that day, chiefly in asking questions about the practices of the smugglers when they used these parts. He gained a great deal of information from the bald-headed jeweller, whom he saw leaning in his shop-door. He asked him if the bracelet had been delivered, and they fell into conversation, watched by the hairdresser opposite, who wished his father had bred him a jeweller.

This jeweller had much to tell of midnight affairs down on the wharf, and landings contrived on the beach amidst a crackling of blunderbuss and pistol. The revenue people, he said, had always been, as they still were, as determined and heroic as their foemen.

'But,' said Captain Jackman, 'I am told that you have no revenue people left here.'

The jeweller answered —

'There is one, I believe, paces the cliff side 'twixt——' And he named two little places on the coast.

'That's to the east'ard,' said the captain.

'Yes, sir. For some unnameable reason, considering they had taken so much trouble in the Devil's Walk, the whole body of the men sailed east.'

'So that further west, and further west still,' said Captain Jackman, 'you'll scarcely find a look-out.'

'I doubt if you'd find one.'

'Why don't they run their goods west, then?' said the captain. 'No look-out is what they want, isn't it?'

'They'd be watched and followed, sir. It is a difficult calling, full of blood and murder. It don't seem worth while, for my part. Some comes off with profits worth naming; but the gains on the whole are poor, and the gibbet's rope is dangling over their heads all the time they're earning their desperate living.'

'So it is,' said the captain, and he strolled across to his little inn.

At six o'clock the table was prepared, and
Captain Jackman was awaiting the arrival
of his guests, who appeared on foot as the
church clock struck the hour.   Miss Conway
was rosy red ; her first words were—

'Captain Jackman, I have not words to
thank you.   This is indeed a glorious
gift.'   And throwing aside her mantle, she
showed that she wore the jewel on her left
arm.

'I know not what the value of my life
expresses, madam,' said Captain Jackman,
smiling as he perceived the bracelet. 'But
if I had fifty lives to save, each one, to put
it prosaically, worth a thousand, that trinket
could not seem more shabby as an illustration
of its worth than it now is.'

'I did not think that our little town
could have turned out so splendid a piece
of jewellery,' said the commander, looking
around him, particularly at the old prints
of sea-fights. 'It is the handsomest thing
of the sort I ever saw, and my daughter
should be obliged to ye.'

'She is, I assure you,' she exclaimed.
'On such charming conditions who would

object to release strangers from smugglers' tunnels ?'

The landlady conducted Miss Conway upstairs, and she came down in a few minutes, delightful in colour, stature, demeanour, and dress. She wore her hair so that it fell thick and low on one side ; the other side was balanced by a handsome comb. A quantity of frills sat upon her neck and shoulders, leaving exposed a portion of her white bosom, which was further sweetened by the late beauty of an autumn flower.

They took their seats. A man waited. It was to be a good dinner, the commander saw.

'I've been taking a look about your neighbourhood,' said Captain Jackman. ' Very pretty, and the sea view spacious, but rather tame, I fear.'

' Yes,' clipped in Miss Conway. ' Those who praise this place when the summer is glowing with roses forget the seven months of winter, the roaring chimneys, the eternal crash of sea, so cold that your marrow hardens to it ! You can't leave your house for the snow, nobody can come to see you, and this is the life my father dedicates his only daughter to !'

But she did not speak in temper. No swell of bosom or sparkle of eye accompanied her words. It seemed indeed as if she merely coquetted with the point, and Captain Jackman noticed it.

'The fact is,' said the commander, fastening his eye on Captain Jackman, 'I am too poor to live anywhere else.'

'I hate poverty,' exclaimed the captain, with a scowl; 'it is the most detestable of human misfortunes. What is meant by being poor? To possess all the desire without the capacity of enjoyment. Fortunately there is no poverty at sea; money is not wanted. There is nothing to buy.'

'You shall not call yourself a poor man here, Captain Jackman,' said Miss Conway, flashing an arch look at him.

'How is a man to make his fortune in this age,' continued the captain, 'now that the wars are ended, and there is nothing to be done in buccaneering and the loose trades? What use, for example, can I put my brig to?'

'You see,' said the commander, 'being a naval man I have very little knowledge of the merchant side of the ocean life.'

'I shall sell her, she is of no use to me,' said the captain, looking at Miss Conway.

'Is she fit to go to sea?' asked the girl.

'She wants about three hundred pounds spent upon her, and where am I to get it?'

The young lady looked down with a face of remorse at the beautiful bracelet upon her wrist. It was a speech in bad taste, yet it did not lessen the beauty of his face nor the agreeable mystery he seemed to carry with him.

'I doubt if you will stop here long,' said the commander. 'Any sea-faring business brought you here, may I venture to ask?'

'None. Nothing but a wish to see if the smugglers had left some booty behind them; and to lounge about this part of the land until my finances advised me to arrive at a decision.'

'You should always be able to get command of a ship, Captain Jackman,' said the girl.

'Not so easy now I have been dismissed for theft.'

'Oh no!' muttered the commander, 'dismissed for a misadventure. Had it been theft, sir, you would not have been here, nor should we be enjoying the splendid dinner you are giving us.'

He tippled down another glass of champagne. Very good champagne it was; his eyes beamed with it and the port, and the hardness had dissolved from his looks, and his face expressed the smiling side of him.

'They'll all understand what my discharge means,' said the captain. 'I had served the owners with heroic honesty, having brought off their lumbering merchantman from a very heavy ugly pirate, right amidships of the Atlantic. We made a running fight of it, and I brought the rogue's foretopgallant mast down. The villain rounded to, and my good friends' bales and tea were saved.'

'They choose to forget that,' said Miss Conway warmly.

'A shipowner,' said the captain, in a soft voice, addressing himself to the girl, 'is by birth a scoundrel, who will not forgive you

one error—one oversight'—his forefinger
flew up in seeming passion—' be your record
the most dutiful, honourable, and lucrative
of them all.'

' I can believe it,' said the commander,
with a loud laugh; ' and yet you are for
choosing the red flag instead of my own
glorious colour.'

' How long were you at sea last voyage?'
asked Miss Conway, whilst the captain
gloomily gazed at the commander.

'Twenty-four months.'

' And you have had command in other
ships ?' she said.

' In several,' he answered.

' You are a young man,' she exclaimed,
whilst her eyes lingered upon his face with
evident delight, ' to have been in command
so long.'

' Shall I tell you a secret, madam ?' said
he, smiling. ' In fact, shall I tell you my
age? Then learn it by this, that I was
twenty when I first took charge of a ship.'

'Very young and very creditable. It
works you out at about thirty,' said the
commander.

The captain bowed as if to a sentence of kindness.

He dined them as sumptuously as the shops of that place could provide: and after dinner they went upstairs to a spinet, where Miss Conway gave them some music. She played very prettily, and sang also. But her singing was not of the fine quality you would have expected in a girl who possessed a voice. Captain Jackman's eyes were riveted to her all the while she sat at the spinet ; and he declined to give heed when the sturdy old commander slung a question across the room to him in the midst of his daughter's performance. A strange old room in a vanished inn ! You can dine on the site, but not in the house. It was probably then a hundred years old, was low pitched, wainscot bright with time, ceiling covered with carvings of flying Cupids and fruits, and the furniture was in keeping, dull, dim, and dusty.

Thus they amused themselves till about half-past eight, during which time the commander and Captain Jackman drank some hot whisky-and-water. They then lighted their pipes and sallied forth, the commander pausing in the bar to sing out in a deep bass voice—

'A very good dinner, Mrs. Davis. I would never wish to sit down to a better.'

The good woman, who had really done her best, dropped curtseys in the fine old English style, coming round out of the bar that she might continue to curtsey, until the lady and gentlemen were in the street.

Commander Conway was by no means anxious that Captain Jackman should see them home; he felt sure he must be tired; he had been on his legs all day; it was a long walk, and then there was the walk back. The captain said he would accompany them part of the way only, and strode on the young lady's left, where the beautiful bracelet was. They talked together, and the commander did not seem to greatly heed; in truth the coming out into this strong fresh air had a little staggered his senses.

'Ours, Captain Jackman, has been a strange meeting,' said the girl. 'I shall never cease praising my judgment for taking a walk on the sands that morning.'

' I owe my life to you,' said he, in a low, somewhat impassioned voice, ' and mean to keep it for you.   Let you marry whom you will, I marry no one but you.'

At this extraordinary speech she walked a little fast, so as to carry her ahead ; but she fell back easily into her place, whilst her father on the other side of the captain was singing, ' The Bowline's Hauled.'

' I would rather not talk of anything of this sort at present,' said the girl, after a prolonged pause.   ' You are not, I hope, returning *very* soon ?'

' Not too soon,' he answered.

' What's that light out there ?' shouted the commander, pointing to the dark and troubled slope of sea.

' A flare of distress,' answered the captain.

They stood looking, talking about the light, which presently disappeared, and when they walked on all three chatted. The conversation was general until Captain Jackman bade farewell to them about half a mile distant from the commander's house.

' I don't like him.   I can't make up my mind to like him,' said the commander, as he trudged with a roll forward towards the square shadow where his own square shadow lived. 'He is liberal with his gifts, and gives a good dinner.'

'And for that he is to be abused !' exclaimed the girl. 'Considering he is a sailor, he is the most perfect gentleman I ever met ; much more so than the rough and cursing creatures you meet with in the navy. He has a beautiful face, and his attention to me that night in the tunnel never shall I forget while my heart beats. You don't seem either to much value the life of your child in your abuse of the man.'

The commander trudged on more rapidly. He was sleepy, and besides, Miss Conway, imperious, sarcastic, overbearing, always conquered the square little fellow, whatever might prove the discussion.

Now for the next two days nothing was seen of Captain Jackman. Miss Conway was mortified and astonished. Could it be possible that the giver of the magnificent bracelet, the partner in their tragic experience under earth, the man who had cleverly run acquaintance into friendship in a single day through a hospitable and sparkling occasion ; could this man, after what he had said to her last night, have slunk away on the coach for a fresh destination, contenting himself with having made a fool of another girl and paid a fair price for his valuable life ?

She walked down the one street, and in and out of it. She walked on to the wharf. She strolled where she thought she would meet him.

If it is false that a girl cannot fall in love at sight with a handsome man, then this tale is a lie, for assuredly Miss Conway could not have been more in love with Captain Jackman had they been betrothed a year. On the third day, however, she was standing at her bedroom window, which gave a clear view of the reach to the crazy rail of the smugglers' hole, when she saw a figure wrapped in a cloak pass the house within gunshot. He did not seem to notice the house, but walked straight on, making apparently for the Devil's Walk. Her heart beat a little fast. She knew him. Should she go out and meet him, and challenge his reason for not calling and proving himself as friendly as he was on the first day ?

She was a young woman with a character as hard as the rock she dwelt on, and she was perfectly fearless in the execution of her ideas. She had been pining for this man. He was out yonder walking. She wanted him ; so she put on her hat, left the house, and followed him.

As she stepped into the road Mrs. Porter came along. Mrs. Porter was a tall, stately, stout lady, the widow of an admiral. She was the very last person that Ada could have wished to see just then.

' Ah, my dear Miss Conway,' she cried, ' I have been on the look-out for you, and meant to have called this very afternoon. What can you tell me about your wonderful night in the Devil's Walk ? And what has become of the beautiful young man you were locked up with ? Oh, fie !'

She shook her head with a succession of odd smirks, and continued—

' They're all saying, if he is a gentleman and can support you, you must marry him.'

' If you knew how I detest the opinions

6

of people you would not force them upon me,' said Ada Conway, looking very darkly at stout Mrs. Porter, and then casting a glance of blazing impatience in the direction of the cloaked figure that seemed to be making for the smugglers' trap.

' But wasn't it shocking ?' continued Mrs. Porter, ' without a light, alone with a man whom you had not seen !'

' But you know the story,' said Ada, with a trifle of arch sarcasm in her tone ; ' why do you want it over again, good Mrs. Porter ?'

' We love to drink from the original spring, that was the admiral's favourite saying. Never trust a story or a report, he would say ; go and talk to the man who figured in it.'

' Well, I shall be seeing you this afternoon perhaps, Mrs. Porter ; meanwhile I'm off for a walk, far beyond your ambling paces ; so farewell.'

She blew the old lady a kiss in the most gracious style of that age, then swept away without another word.

The commander, standing in his window,

caught sight of her, and rushed round out of doors slap into the arms of Mrs. Porter.

'Why, commander,' began the lady, 'this is an unexpected pleasure indeed.'

'Hi! Ada, where are you going?' shouted the old seaman, in his roughest voice.

Ada half turned her face and made an ironic flourish of farewell, but spoke no word.

'She's after that man,' said the commander, with a black look in the direction of the becloaked figure. 'She's fallen head over heels in love with him, and he must either be forced out of the place or——'

'What, Captain Conway—do say what?' cried Mrs. Porter.

'Or battened down in the Devil's Walk to cry again from help for another pretty woman.'

'Give that out, and the sands will not want paraders,' said humorous Mrs. Porter.

They stood conversing. The commander was detained by the lady who would have hindered Ada. So even Mrs. Porters have their uses. Meanwhile the girl, whose heart her father knew, rough old seaman as he was, was stepping out briskly, literally in chase of the man she was determined to have a meeting with. She was only slightly vexed that her father had seen him pass; she would rather her father had been asleep in an armchair, or shaving himself in his bedroom, which did not overlook Captain Jackman. Jackman took the ground with an actor's tread; her pursuit carried the sound of her footsteps to his ears; he turned, looked, started with pleasure and astonishment, and ran forward to meet the young lady.

' I am surprised,' she cried, with her face red as fire, ' that you should think it friendly to stay away from our house for two days, never to inquire how I was after that barbarous night underground, and now to give the go-by to our home.'

He held her hand whilst she spoke, and answered, ' I was away yesterday, madam; but in any case I should not have called. I saw dislike in your father's face.'

' My father dislikes everything that is not aged and rotten. He buys old books, and if they're printed in characters he can't read, so much the better. He believes in the ships of a hundred years ago, and laughs with a sneer at the line-of-battle ships of to-day. He has lived for years a stagnant life; it is a pond on which all sorts of ugly weeds grow and blow. Do not concern yourself with his dislike. Where are you going?'

'I was going merely for a stroll as far as the entrance to the Devil's Walk. Frankly, in expectation of meeting you,' he answered, with his eyes filled with active love fastened upon hers.

The colour sank out of her face when she noticed that look. She was loved, and the truth went to her heart.

'We will walk as far as the smugglers' hole and then return,' said she, taking possession of him with an easy spirit that made him adore her grace, and wonder where she had learnt her engaging airs.

'Where did you go yesterday?'

'To a little village ten miles down the coast,' he answered. 'Did you notice the other night as we walked home the light of a flare upon the sea?'

' Yes.'

' Well, it proved, as I suspected, a distress signal. It was burnt on a roughly con-structed raft which managed, by dint of boards and other contrivances, to strand itself in safety. They were eight men. I heard the tale in your town. They were smugglers who had lost their vessel by a butt-end starting. They trudged to the little village and were put up there, and are still there.'

' Are you a smuggler?' she exclaimed, looking with vivid keenness into his face.

' I am Captain Jackman,' he answered, bowing and laughing. ' No smuggler, but no scorner of the trade. I went yesterday to see those men, and think that I have secured the services of five of the stoutest of them.'

' What! for smuggling, Captain Jack-man?'

' No, for a sweeter, swifter, and richer pursuit, madam, which I would whisper in your ear with feverish delight, sure of your sympathy and approval, if this hand '—he took it—' were mine.'

She began to tremble. She was being

made love to in reality. She was a little
frightened. Greatly she enjoyed the situation she had placed herself in, and said, with
her head hanging down—

' My father must know what we do.'

' You want me to consult with him about
our marriage ?'

' Oh, not so fast, Captain Jackman,' she
exclaimed, colouring with delight at his
impetuosity.

' He will never give his consent,' he said.
' He doesn't like merchantmen. He hates
poor men, and so I do. He'll talk of our
three or four days of acquaintanceship, and
heap every objection he can find and create.'

' And then,' said the girl, speaking firmly,
with her face of beauty improved with an
expression of decision almost feverish in its
impulse, ' there is a second road.' She
looked at him boldly.

' Why not take that second road at once ?'
he exclaimed softly, passing his arm through
hers; and the love-sick girl let it lie there,
and cherished it.

' No, Captain Jackman——'

' Walter.'

'Walter, then, we will be truthful and above-board; you shall go and ask my father's consent and answer his questions. He may not refuse. That would be so much better. For him now, and for memory for us in after years.'

'I would do whatever you wish. I have no queen but you,' answered Captain Jackman, who certainly was as much in love with the girl as she with him.

'How long are you stopping in this place?' she asked.

'I am at your service,' he replied.

'Well,' said she, speaking rapidly, 'we must be seen together for some days. You must call upon the commander and talk of anything but me. Then come when I am in the house by pre-arrangement, and the matter can be dealt with. Meanwhile I should like to know your reason for picking up sailors.'

'I have a scheme in my head,' he answered.

'So I suppose,' she replied; 'and I engage that it concerns your brig.'

'You are a witch, miss,' he exclaimed,

smiling at her. 'Of course, the knowing
that I am here seeking sailors did not put
that into your head.'

'I knew nothing about that until just
now,' she answered; 'but fancies rose in my
head when you talked of the brig whilst we
were together.'

They approached, and stood at the broken
rail that fenced the stone.

'I hope you are not going below!' cried
Miss Conway, flashing her eyes with command upon him. 'If you do, I protest I
will bolt you down and leave another to
release you. How many candles have you
got?'

'I am not going to enter those caverns,
believe me,' he answered. 'At the same
time, I am wondering whether I could find
an abandoned cave along this cliff with an
outlet to the sea. There should be plenty.
I do not want to go east; I mean to give the
Downs, with the shipping and the men-of-
war, a wide berth. Have you ever heard of
such a cave?'

'Never. It may be found,' she answered.
'So you are going to turn smuggler? I

could not marry a man whose body might be hanging in air within a month of the wedding.'

'I vow I am not going to turn smuggler. I purpose something infinitely more noble and more shining. I am a decayed gentleman, and a decayed gentleman must live. They won't find me a berth ashore, so I must go to sea, where I intend, in my brig, in a week or ten days, or say three weeks, to make a fortune.'

'Father can never object to that scheme,' exclaimed the girl; 'he admires commercial adventures, and would greatly respect you for loading your ship and sailing in search of fortune.'

They continued to converse as they walked in the direction of the commander's house. Captain Jackman was mysterious, but his looks were eloquent. Ada's eyes dredged the captain's face for a hint, but got no idea. Suddenly he paused, and said—

'Here we must part.'

'In view of my father's house! Certainly not. You will step in, Walter, and dine with us.'

He seemed to shrink, with smiles full of courtesy.

'Oh,' said she, lightly catching hold of his cloak and bearing him towards the cottage, 'you are refusing a lady. I know you have no other engagement. Pray step in, and dine with us.'

Almost unconsciously the stouthearted, manly, handsome Captain Jackman found himself in the commander's garden, walking towards the commander's house; and now there was the commander himself approaching them from his back garden, wearing carpet slippers and holding a broom, with which he had been attending to his fowls.

'Oh, good morning, Captain Jackman,' he shouted, as if he were hailing the masthead of a ship. 'Those Devil's Walks of ours seem to have exercised a pleasant fascination over your mind.'

'What do you think, father? Captain Jackman was actually passing this house not long ago without intending to call.'

'Captain Jackman's ideas of reserve may be different from yours,' said the commander.

'Yes,' she cried quickly; 'and after

luncheon I am going to show him about the place.'

'The place' was to be viewed, every street and alley, in an hour, and Captain Jackman had now been some three or four days in these parts exploring. The commander stared at the cool turn his daughter gave to things, and muttering, 'Oh yes, sir ; you'll stop to lunch, I hope, you'll stop to lunch,' he shuffled out on his slippered feet to put away his broom.

CHAPTER IV.

THE PROPOSAL.

ONE afternoon, a week after Captain Jackman had lunched at Battle Lodge, as the commander had tremendously named his trifling villa, Miss Conway was pacing her bedroom with impatient feet, slanting an eye, eloquent of purpose that had waxed almost into temper, over the old-fashioned, puckered blinds which concealed the interior of the room from the roadway leading to the town.

At this same hour, the commander, who was red in the face from having sat beside the fire, was musing over a letter in his hand.

'What can he want?' he thought, as he strutted from the table to the window to and fro. 'Does he hope to borrow money? I have not a farthing to lend him, and should at once insist upon returning his bracelet. Is he seeking some situation here? There is nothing vacant down at the wharf, or upon the coast, anyway, that I have heard of, though I should be glad to oblige a man who acted as he did towards my daughter in a delicate and difficult situation. I would oblige him, certainly, I have thanked him merely. He, on the other hand, has given us a noble bracelet and a magnificent dinner.'

The letter sank in his hand. The bigoted old fool stared hard into the fire. These wonderful old people, who believe in nothing but the dead thing in the ships they've sailed in, in the pap-bottle they sucked at, do not seem able to see round the corner, where the live thing absolute, and no nonsense about it, is always coming.

The hall bell clanked, and presently the servant admitted Captain Jackman. There were the usual salutations.

'So you are still amusing yourself in these parts,' said the commander. 'Pray be seated, captain.'

'It answers my purpose to linger,' answered Captain Jackman coolly.

And the commander had to own that the fellow looked uncommonly handsome, with a gentleman-like character about his beauty, which was promise of a good record.

'I thought,' said the commander, with a harsh, uneasy laugh, 'that you were here only to inspect the Devil's Walk.'

'Surely, sir, my reasons for remaining here need be known to myself only, I hope.'

'Quite so,' said the commander largely.

'But I intend,' continued Captain Jackman, 'to make you a sharer in the business of my detention, by telling you that the letter you hold is to ask you for the hand of your daughter Ada.'

'No, sir, never!' shouted the commander.

'Softly, commander. You do not seem to consider that we are truly in love, that she is over age, and—— '

'And what, sir?' bawled Commander Conway.

The captain smiled.

'Keep seated,' said the commander.

He seated himself by the fire, and now the talk flowed.

'This is my only daughter, do you see,'

said the silver-headed old man. 'I hope you do not mean to take her from me.'

'Every girl needs a father at the start, and a husband afterwards,' said Captain Jackman. 'This girl is too beautiful and noble in spirit to be allowed to languish on top of a cliff within sight of a single scene of the sea. Young women like pleasures—music, the dance, the theatre, the opera—they do not care for nothing but windmills and fishing-boats—— ' He was proceeding.

'Hold, sir !' shouted the commander. 'What portion of all this glory could you display to my daughter ?'

'I will take her off a cliff to start with, commander, and anchor her close to the sights which are worth seeing.'

'What are your means ? Can you support my daughter without obliging me to put my hand in my pocket ?'

'I shall not call upon you for a bad sixpence,' answered Captain Jackman, with a lofty toss of his head.

The commander stared hard at him, and breathed short, then burst forth—

'But how do I know who you are ? You

get locked up in a cave with my daughter, fall in love with her inside of a fortnight, and propose for her hand. I am thunder-struck. Marriage is a slow and solemn thing—a contract that is not to be thundered through as though a hurricane of need blew astern of it. You have told us your parents are dead, and I have no doubt, sir, from the sample they have left in their offspring, that they were in the highest degree respectable ; but they were strangers. I never contem-plated a marriage of this sort. You may have relations my daughter may find extremely degrading to her.'

'You should not talk thus without know-ing,' said Captain Jackman, starting on his chair, and looking very fiery and disdainful. 'It is not customary, I think, to sweep the circle of the relations of a lady whose hand we propose for, otherwise——' He coughed.

'What does that cough signify, sir?'

'Mr. Fortt!'

The commander coloured, and looked viciously at the captain, but made no reply ; in fact, he had no reply to make ; for Captain Jackman, in probing and prowling

7

about and asking questions, had got to hear
that Fortt, who was a retired dairyman and
a good-looking man with strong whiskers,
had married Conway's sister, and was living
with her in a handsome villa. The commander was not, by this marriage, to be
driven from his guns. He stuck to his
home, but he never approached the Fortts'
house, nor had a word or a look for his
sister and her man if he met them. On the
other hand, Miss Conway regularly visited
her uncle and aunt, and occasionally made
excursions with them to a considerable
distance, such as Canterbury and London.

At this instant she entered. She leapt in
a graceful bound from the bottom step of the
short flight into the room, giving her body
as many swings, though always of a stately
sort, as you would expect to see in some
lively princess on her entrance.

' Why, Captain Jackman !' she cried with
well-assumed amazement at his presence, as
if she had not watched him coming, as if
she had not seen him turn the corner to
ring the hall bell, as if she had not heard, at
the head of the short staircase, the loud

conversation that had followed on his admission. 'This, our sailors here would say, is a sight for sore eyes. We are bears in a cage to you; and you do not love bears.'

'I have come, madam,' said Captain Jackman, 'to speak to the commander on a subject which must needs be of deep interest to us both.'

'What is it?' she cried, beginning to heave her breast, and looking at her father.

'Captain Jackman's called to ask for your hand in marriage,' said the commander.

'Well?' said the girl.

'I cannot give my consent.'

'Why not? Captain Jackman is a man of as good degree as you. He is a gentleman to the very heels of him, don't you know. I love him; and you *must* consent!'

'There is a mystery,' said Commander Conway, clasping his gouty hands upon his portly waistcoat, 'that troubles me, and excites dislike. What was he doing in the Devil's Walk?'

'Curiosity, sir. I have answered that. Curiosity took me there.'

'It is not satisfactory to me that the captain should have been dismissed his ship for having been innocently robbed of fifteen hundred pounds.'

'I would advise you to say no more in respect of that,' said the captain, stepping so as to confront Commander Conway. 'I am a man to force you to apologise for your infamous insinuation by carrying you to London, and compelling you to face the owners themselves.'

'I wish you to say nothing more about it,' exclaimed the commander, with an angry motion of his arm, the fist of which looked to be locked. 'What I want you both to understand is, I cannot approve of, and therefore cannot sanction, the marriage of my daughter to a stranger who had no existence to us a few days ago; who has not explained how he is to support his wife when he marries her—whether he intends to go to sea and carry his wife with him, or leave her ashore. If ashore, what sort of home can his means afford her? For, sir,' he said, looking up at the captain, who still stood in front of him, 'we know that a

master in the merchant service is not paid
wages which a wise sailor would dream ot
getting married on. And at present you
have no ship, no employ, no more prob-
abilities of work than other people walking
about the docks—all excepting a brig,
upon which heirloom I make you my
compliments.' And he bowed with a
sarcastic air.

'There is not the slightest use,' Captain
Jackman replied, 'in answering your questions, unless you intend to give us your
sanction.'

Ada, fast breathing, eyes glittering,
nostrils swelling, stepped round and stood
beside her man—a handsome pair.

'You may depend upon it,' continued the
captain, 'that if I marry this lady, I shall
not trouble you; on the contrary, I think it
more likely that you will trouble me.'

'What do you mean, sir?' shouted the
commander.

'I have a golden scheme, and it will
come off,' said Captain Jackman, with a
singular smile lighting up his face.

The commander was silent for at least a

minute. A minute is a long time of silence on an occasion of this sort. During the pause he eyed Jackman with a gaze of corkscrews and screwdrivers.

'I see how it is, father,' said Miss Conway, in a voice of bitter contempt, and with a manner daringly defiant. 'You mean to keep me at home all my life—or your life, which may be long, for you take good care of yourself. You mean that I should become a wrinkled old maid, without hopes of a husband, without a chance of getting away from this sickeningly dull hole, merely because it suits you, and it is convenient to you to keep me at home as a companion. You do not love to be alone. I would bear you company willingly,' she cried, with enlarged nostril, 'to your grave, though it should make me sixty years of age, if it were not for your selfishness.'

'Sir,' said the commander, 'you perceive what sort of a young lady you wish to clasp to your heart as a life partner.'

'Have I your consent to our marriage,' answered the tall, handsome Jackman, looking down at Commander Conway with a barely visible curve of contempt at either corner of his mouth.

'He would deny me a sight of life,' shrieked the girl almost hysterically. 'I am to gaze, by his command, on nothing but the ocean. We go nowhere. I take lonely walks. You saw me on one of those lonely walks, Captain Jackman, and I am thankful to remember that I saved your life. My father is selfish, and does not enter into the feelings of the young. *He* has lived, and we too must live and see life. This gentleman loves me,' she said, laying her hand with fine grace upon the captain's shoulder, and looking at her father with an expression of desperation in her beauty, 'and I love him, and we shall be married.'

The commander, not perhaps relishing the being seated whilst these two continued to tower over him, sprang up and stepped across to the other side of the table.

'You'll not marry with my consent,' he exclaimed, 'until I learn more of this gentleman's antecedents, connections, career. I don't want certificates of conduct,' he added with an arch sneer. 'I want to

know is this man who has made a bid for
my family a gentleman ?   Next let me be
satisfied as to the ways and means of this
business.   He is flinging his money gener-
ously about down here ; he should have
plenty.   Will you not tell me how much
you have ?'

'I have told you that I'm a poor man ;
but that I have an occupation, and meanwhile
a brilliant scheme.'

'Submit it,' shouted the commander.

Captain Jackman shook his head slowly.

'And you think I'm going to sanction
your marrying my daughter—to such a man
as you ?   What is your mystery ?   You
shall hire the Devil's Walk, and spend a
little money on decorating it, and support
my daughter on the sixpences you take.'
The commander laughed harshly.   'There
is no room in this house, I beg to assure
you, for two families ; and that being so,
and as you decline to give me any satisfaction
as to your antecedents, and your capability
of supporting a wife, I absolutely decline to
sanction your marriage.'

Saying which he gave Captain Jackman a

stiff bow, left the room, and marched very
creakily upstairs. The lovers looked at each
other in silence, and then the captain kissed
the girl's forehead. Tears were in her
eyes.

'There is the other way,' said he, in a
soft voice. 'Unnatural thoughts should be
opposed by unnatural deeds. I am a gentleman—as much so as he. He knows it. He
is prejudiced. He does not like my being
fallen in with in that cave. He does not
like the idea of having a master in the
merchant service for a son-in-law. Ada,'
he whispered, 'he will never consent, but
there is the other way.' He made a move-
ment so as to leave the house.

'You have said nothing about our future
arrangements,' she cried.

'Everything now depends upon you,' he
answered, very softly. 'There is the other
way, my dearest,' he again whispered with
great significance, and a look that beamed
with love.

'Stay, I will put on my hat and walk into
the town with you. We can arrange at our
hearts' will as we go.'

Commander Conway stood at his window overlooking the road, and witnessed this couple's departure. He was deeply incensed. But, like all fathers thus placed with an active, determined daughter who would marry a bagman sooner than remain un-wedded, all that he could do was to gesticu-late, and all that he could say was, *no*, with the emphasis of the rolling sea, and then sit down upon that ' no ' and await the conse-quences of his heart-breaking command.

He saw old Mr. Leaddropper, a retired pilot of the Trinity House, a man with very arched legs, and a full August moon of face, and long shoes with buckles. This man pulled off his round hat to Miss Conway as they passed, and called out—

' Is father at home, missie ?'

' Ay, you'll find him at home,' answered the girl.

Old Leaddropper made several turns with his head after he had got the couple astern, in order to view Captain Jackman. He had heard of this gentleman from his great friend Captain Burgoyne, an old East Indiaman, but had not seen him. Meanwhile Com-

mander Conway at his bedroom window saw
Leaddropper coming, and watched with
mingled emotions the frequent looks the
bow-legged pilot cast behind him.

'How do you do, Conway?' said Leaddropper, entering the house, as the commander descended the stairs.   'Fine gal that
of yours !'

He walked into the dining-room.   The
commander followed him.

'Oh, that I was the man I looked, and
felt, when the last century was eighty !'   He
seated himself.

'You were not just hatched even at that,'
said the commander, walking up and down
the little room.   'What's the news?'

'For my part I've got not a stroke,' said
the old pilot, blandly following with motions
of his blood-stained eyes the movements of
the commander, as he placed a decanter of
rum upon the table, together with a jug of
water and tumblers taken from the sideboard.

'Help yourself,' said the commander.

The pilot did so.   The commander took
a drop, lighted his pipe, and the pilot drank
his health.

'Not a stroke of news,' continued old Leaddropper. 'But stay ! Blamed if there isn't a talk of some one going about working up a crew out of our little town.'

'That'll be Jackman,' said the commander. 'Certain. What can he want a crew for, and why is he found in the Devil's Walk ?'

'Was that the man that I saw your daughter walking with just now ?' inquired the pilot.

The commander let fall a surly nod.

'If so, he's a precious good-looking young man, with that sort of eye which tells of a right heart, so I think. His behaviour to your daughter in them vaults that night was that of a gentleman.'

'Have you come up at anybody's urgent request to do a bit of special pleading with me, Leaddropper?' exclaimed the commander, looking a little darkly upon his friend.

'What do you mean ?'

'I suppose you know,' said the commander, 'that that gentleman, who styles himself Captain Jackman, wants to obtain

my sanction to his marriage to my
daughter ?'

'How should I know ?' said the pilot,
draining his glass, and looking at the
decanter. 'But if it be as you say, where's
the harm ? What's the objection ? If your
gal were mine I should reckon her lucky to
get into tow with one of the handsomest
gentlemen I ever clapped my eyes on.'

'Blast the handsomest gentleman ! How
can a man support a wife on his looks ?
This handsome gentleman has nothing
saving apparently some loose gold '—and
here he spoke with a curious intonation—
'which he is glad to sling about him in this
quiet spot, at the rate of forty-five pounds a
go. Stay !' he added, confused by his own
meanness. 'He has a brig, but without
capital, without a crew, without evidently
any disposition to make use of the brig.
How shall she count in his list of effects ?'

'Young people must have a chance,' said
the pilot. 'Parents are always for opposing
as *they* were opposed ; but the fakes come
out of the coil all the same, and there's no
singing out of " avast !" to the sculler whose

boat has got the end of the rope. How's
your gal, your very fine gal, going to get
married down here? Who's to admire her?
Who's to see her? Naturally, when one
comes along who has eyes, he desires her,
Conway ; and so should I, my friend, if I
could slide my life back thirty year.'

'What have you heard about this collecting of men for a crew?' asked the commander. 'Is there some reference to his
brig in this job? But why should he come
down all these leagues from London for
men? What's being said about my daughter?'

'Nothing that's reached my ears. Nothing
that could annoy ye, anyway,' said the old
pilot. 'I did hear that they were likely to
be engaged because of their being locked up
all night under the earth alone. Some
fathers would feel a little sensitive on this
matter. You don't seem to have taken it to
heart, commander ;' and the pilot flourished
his glass at his mouth, and put it down with
a gesture eloquent of ' no more.'

'Am I to be told,' cried the commander,
whisking round upon the pilot, and taking
aim at him with the stem of his pipe, ' that

every one who saves the life of another must
marry 'em ?   Why, the penalty might be
regarded as so violent there'd be no life-
saving at all.   A young man on the sea-shore
would say, " I see a girl drowning; never do
to save her; most indelicate for her to be
seen lying in my arms in her bathing-gown !"
Nothing but marriage could rescue the lady
from the very compromising situation the
gentleman, by saving her life, had placed
her in.'

Leaddropper sniggered.

Whilst these two old sailors were conversing in the little square cottage on the
top of the tall cliffs, Captain Jackman and
Ada Conway were slowly making their way
towards the town.   The flash of the sea far
down, the guns of the sea low down, the
white lightning of the gulls' flight went with
them; and with them rode a pleasant pano-
rama of shipping ; a line-of-battle ship was
making her way up Channel; she hung
sullen, and tossed with massive plunge,
heaving about her the foam of a dozen
breaking seas; a smart little schooner, with
masts like fishing-rods, sitting low and almost

level, save where her bow struck for domination in an abrupt leap of sheer, was cutting through her own yeast ; others were glorious with the light and the life, and all that the ocean has of beauty to confer upon the fabrics which sail upon it and trust it ; but none of these things did the lovers take heed of.

Probably Jackman had had enough of the sea and its pictures, and nothing short of a whirlpool or a lightning-clothed disaster, full of foam and rolling peals, was likely to court Miss Conway's eye to that wide blue flashing breast.

'Ada,' said Jackman, 'your father will not give his consent. That's as certain to me as that it is I that am talking to you.'

'Why will not he give me my way ?' she cried. 'It's hard to have to take it—to leave an old father. Yet he binds me to him by nothing ; we see little or nothing of each other. I am a convenience as mistress of his house. But I am not mistress, and every day makes me feel the want of independence.'

'Will you trust yourself with me in the little parlour of the "Faithful Heart"?' said the captain, after a short pause. 'I have a project I want to talk to you about.'

'After the Devil's Walk!' she cried, with spirit. 'After that, Walter, I think I should be able to trust you anywhere.'

'Come to the little inn!'

They walked down the broad, steep street, speaking little. Those who knew Miss Conway bowed with arch looks. Not often was a marriage celebrated in that steep little town. A good-looking young man straying into the place was viewed rather with astonishment than with desire. And if ever the desire came it was promptly ended by the good-looking young man's disappearance.

Here now was undoubtedly a good-looking couple, unquestionably engaged to be married; and friends bowed archly, and others stared. They arrived at the 'Faithful Heart' and entered. Captain Jackman conducted the young lady upstairs to the little parlour in which she had played the

8

spinet that night the three had dined together.   The captain was advancing to grasp
the bell-rope.

' What do you want?' said Ada.

' Some refreshments for you.'

' Nothing, absolutely.   Leave that bell
alone, be as swift as possible, come and sit
here on this sofa beside me, and tell me your
secret—the secret, I presume, on which we
are to get married—that is to say, on which
we are to run away, as I too certainly feel
it must come to.'

She spoke in hard words, but in a love-
sweetened voice, and extended her hand to
bring him to her.   He kissed her brow
as though she was a saint and he adored
her.

' To start with, Ada, I am going to tell
you what I never intended to hint at until
we were man and wife, when our lives and
interests should be identical.   But your
father's stubbornness must determine us, we
must elope.   Now, before we do that, it is
my duty to reveal myself in full.   I have
called myself a gentleman, Ada ; to you I
shall endeavour to prove myself one.'

'I need no further proofs,' she answered, looking at him with a smile. 'What is this scheme, dear, which is to prove so golden, and which is to win my father's congratulations?'

The captain laughed.

'I doubt,' he answered, 'if he is of the *so sweet, so delighted, I am sure,* type of men.'

'The scheme!' said the girl earnestly.

'Ada, I must tell you here now what I have sometimes told you before. I am poor —a poor sailor, a stone-broke seaman with a hatred of his calling. I have been dismissed from my ship for a theft, and I look upon myself as lost. No firms owning such vessels as my dignity would suffer me to command would employ me. I am utterly poor—and thirty, and must make my fortune by a *coup* or end my existence.'

'You need not talk like that.'

'The comfortable grave is better than destitution, better than the cold winter's night and the thrust of the night-watch.'

'Your scheme, dear!'

'You have heard me speak of the little

vessel that is lying in the East India Docks. You also know that I have been engaged whilst here in adding to the crew I desire to collect for her.'

'You mean to go to sea in that ship?' she asked eagerly.

'Certainly, and shortly, and on what errand do you suppose, Ada? I mean to be a gentleman,' he continued, smiling with a rather hard expression, 'and I am determined to carry that calling handsomely. Now, listen, my love. Frequently from Lisbon and Cadiz the Spanish and Portuguese merchants are shipping heavy consignments in gold to the Spice and other Islands. I can ascertain the sailing of those ships, and gather their lading.'

The girl began to eye him with a crooked brow, yet with sparkling eyes.

'There is a fortune floating for a man in any one of those craft, and it is my idea, nay, it is my intention, to gut some stately galloon of her precious metal, and retire ashore upon it, living as a fine gentleman with you, Ada.'

'If they catch you, you'll be hanged,' said

the girl, bending her dark brows at him.
'For what you propose to attempt is piracy,
and the pirate is one of those dangling figures
which revolve in irons, and strike horror into
the wayfarer.'

'I am aware that they hang pirates. I
am also aware,' said Captain Jackman, 'that
I must either make my fortune or end my
life. I choose the former. It can be done,
and easily done, in spite, dearest, of your
beautiful staring face of wonder. I intend to
equip my brig with certain artillery, which
shall lie hidden until we get to sea. We
bend sail and reeve all gear in dock, and
blow out quietly with a few of the hands.
As we sail down the Channel, we touch and
pick up portions of the crew which I have
engaged or which remain to be engaged. I
am now in possession of one of the smartest
and fastest brigs afloat, newly coppered to
the bends, liberally armed, with boats at her
davits and the spare rig of a brigantine upon
the booms, which I have contrived by an
arrangement of the maintop.'

'And you mean to go to sea in this
vessel to plunder ships?' said Ada.

'Yes. Are you shocked ?' he exclaimed tenderly.

'Not even if you had resolved to become a smuggler—something surely lower than a pirate.'

'I shall be a pirate for a few days only,' said he, laughing. 'Gentlemen have taken to the road and lived very handsomely upon the purses they have collected. Why should not a gentleman take to the sea, gather together by a like sort of collection from various trading ships such a sum as he might suppose would suffice his wants, and sail away—either home or abroad, according to the needs of his safety ?'

'It is quite true,' said the girl, whose surprise was fast fading out of her striking face, and who looked with the eyes of love at the captain as he talked, 'that gentlemen have taken to the road for a living. One got hanged. He had been a squire in Warwickshire. I have heard my father speak of a man who lived as a gentleman —who, indeed, was so ; he was discovered to have supported his family of a wife and one or two children by going out upon the highway with a brace of pistols and a mask. He would have been taken; but whilst they were thundering at his door he fell dead of heart disease, through excitement, grief, and shame.'

She allowed her eyes to linger upon his whilst she pronounced these closing words.

'All the chances will be upon our side,' said he, speaking with boyish delight, since he seemed to find a sympathy kindling in the girl with his scheme. 'The only risks I run will be from my own men. I believe I shall be easily able to overcome that difficulty.'

'You will have to confess your business to them,' she said.

'Certainly,' he answered. 'But none yet suspect it. A tall merchant ship unarmed, well laden with goods of which I shall have received notice, sails very stately out of the port, say, of Lisbon. She has a barrel or two of money in her lazarette for the planters of the Portuguese settlements. She has forty men before the mast, and twenty in officers and idlers abaft it. Presently a white gleam is seen by the light of the moon. No notice

is taken. Why should notice be taken ?
There are no pirates in those western seas
so close aboard the coast. I wear, or tack
ship, run my brig alongside, and board her,
whilst half her people are asleep below.'

Ada smiled whilst she listened to her
lover's repetition of the fantastic sketch she
herself had drawn at her father's breakfast-
table.

'We batten everybody down, leaving one
to liberate the people after, then search for
our needs, send the booty over the side into
the brig, and sail away, Ada—and sail away,
my love, a rich, unknown ship. What can
they call us ? How can the terrified dagos
describe us ? A British crew won't stop for
an enemy to look. She is a brig. They
will know that ; but should she leave port
again, she will be a brigantine. What
could they report ? And what do you think
of my scheme ?'

'It is bold, possible, and dishonourable,'
she said, with a subtle note of triumph in
her voice, and the same high, encouraging
colour of sympathy in her face.

'It is not dishonourable,' said he calmly,

'for an Englishman to rob a foreigner upon the seas where the Englishman has himself been most atrociously looted by most of the nations you can name. I must live by a dishonourable income or die by my own hand.'

He made a step to her, and taking her cheeks, gently lifted her face to his, and said—

'My life is now in your hands. I have confessed all to the woman I love, have ever loved, shall ever love. Knowing my scheme, Ada, will you be my wife?'

There was no hesitation in her answer. 'Yes.'

How could she resist his pleading presence, his manly candour with her, the love that lighted his eyes, the love that was now the single impulse of her life? Worthier women for more worthless men have consented to go to the devil.

He kissed and released her face, and said, as he stepped from her—

'I shall be a proud man when I have you by my side. We ought to get married soon, Ada. Will you leave it to me to make all the arrangements, writing under cover to you at this little inn ?'

'Yes,' she answered. 'Father will never consent. Only think if he should get to hear——' She stopped herself.

The captain laughed. 'I must be off to the west,' said he, 'in a day or two, in search of suitable vaults and a temporary home for you.'

The girl arched her black eyebrows, and her lips fixed themselves in an expression of determination.

'I must,' he continued, 'discover if there are any smugglers' vaults on the Cornwall coast. I want to get as near to the Land's End as possible. You, without suspicion, can make inquiries amongst the men on the wharf and elsewhere.'

'Will you return for the news I receive ?'

'You must write——' And he wrote an address on the fly-leaf of a pocket-book which he gave to her. 'That till next Monday.'

Then, after making arrangements for his writing to her from London, whither he would have to repair for the further equipment of his little ship when he had done his business down west, he took her in his arms, kissed her, and conducted her from the inn.

CHAPTER V.

AT the date of this story, remote as it is, the East India Docks were much as they now are, saving in certain non-essential points, such as the funnel. Dismount the funnel of to-day, and leave the pole-mast schooner rigged with its derrick, and old men of that age, stumbling with flapping skirts and breast-wide hats, would scarcely witness a change.

On a certain day, when, strange to relate, it was fine weather over the Isle of Dogs, a great plenty of tall and stately ships lay in these East India Docks. Some were loaded deep, and ready for the voyage, fresh with paint, and sparkling with the glory of glittering gilt and radiant counters. Some had but recently hauled in, and showed signs of bitter conflict with the ocean; the red stain drained from the bolt, the bolt was twisted, a length of bulwark was stove.

Up in a corner, inside a fine West India-man, lay Captain Jackman's brig, about which we have already heard a great deal. His father had owned her, and when young had sailed her, and in his time had made money out of her. He bequeathed the little ship to his son Walter, praying that he would take good care of her, as she inherited several fine traditions, was the noblest sailer of all vessels so rigged that ever he had known, and was a magnificent sea boat.

They were painting her black this day; the parts the painters over the side were covering showed of a dirty white. They were likewise sending her yards aloft, and Captain Jackman, as he came along, could not fail to admire the exquisite precision with which the two masts were stayed. He saw speed in their gentle devoir to the bow; he stopped a minute to watch the painters, and to observe the man who was gilding the small figure-head under the long bowsprit over-laid by the jibbooms. He then went on board.

A man dressed in the style of a master-rigger touched his cap on Jackman's entering. A number of hands were in motion about the decks; the little ship was full of business, there had evidently come some final call.

'Well, Tomson,' said Jackman to the man who had touched his cap, 'how are you getting on ?'

'Smartly, sir. Your ship shall be ready for you by your date.'

'Can you contrive to convert that main-top into a schooner rig on emergency ?'

'It can be done, sir.'

As the man spoke these words a messenger came over the gangway and handed the captain a letter. He looked at it, slightly changed colour, and walked right aft, where he was alone. The missive, dated from Commander Conway's house, ran thus—

'MY DEAREST WALTER,
        'I hasten to communicate what I hope will prove a useful piece of intelligence

to you. I have been busily making inquiries about disused smugglers' caves down west, with this result. A sailor named Butler came to me yesterday and said he could produce a man, a rather old man, who could furnish information of a curious cave striking from the roof of the cliff to the wash of the sea. It had not been used since 1807, but you can still at ebb walk from the lower orifice on to the beach, and from the next to the lower orifice you can use a boat whilst the tide is making. I will give you the name and address of the owner on your passing through here, as *that* you must do, for it is my particular desire to see you.

' How far has been your advance in this tremendous business ? Pray do not be communicative to strangers. Are not you apt to be a little candid, and to forget that you were so ? The sailor is a character of perfect sensibility, and he has to carefully guard himself against the worldly people he meets ashore—people who will wring his business out of him, and then, if they can make no use of it, fling it to the dogs. Oh, I quite forgot to say in its place that with these subterranean stairs to the sea is associated a little house that stands close to the main entrance, and you can enter it by a man-hole in the house itself. This might prove useful.

' The district is very desolate, the old man told me—a livid, gale-swept moor with no habitation within a good drive. Revenue people, I am informed, are occasionally seen on that part of the coast, but at such long intervals that they might as well be viewed as strange objects of interest. The revenue cutter may also be seen plying off the land ; but her business would seem to be far higher up.

' I am never weary of admiring your glorious gift. Oh, how beautifully it sparkles by candlelight ! My father's mood is as stern and unbending as ever. I believe he would strike me if I even referred to you. I heard Captain Burgoyne asking, in his coarse way, which the commander relishes, " Don't you want your wench to get married at all, Conway ? Suppose you pop off on a sudden—and I may tell you I've long viewed with anxiety that stout throat and immense

chest of yours—what is your girl to do?
She is unmated.   Who is to look after her?
And she is pre-eminently one of those young
parties who need looking after."

'I was listening greedily halfway up the
stairs, down which I was coming at the
moment of arrest, dressed for a visit.   My
father answered, " I am not going to have
for a son-in-law a man who may end his
career at the gibbet within the next month."
" Chaw ! you dined with him.   He was an
honourable gentleman then."   My father
began to bluster.   Here stupid Mrs. Dove
came creaking downstairs, and called to me
to go into the hall and turn that she might
admire me.

' All the same I managed to catch a frag-
ment of Captain Burgoyne's remark.   " He
is good-looking.   He is qualified to command
a ship.   He can handle a ship when he
pleases."   " No," thundered the commander
—and as I passed through the hall door,
after giving Mrs. Dove a nod—" Are you,"
shouted my father, " going to be satisfied
with his cool statement of that large loss of
money ?"

' I could not linger, as Mrs. Dove was watching me with affectionate interest from the staircase, and so I left the house.   Nothing that my father can say can affect my love. I am dying to be your wife, and you will find me ready at the first signal you hoist. Wherever you are I am, in spirit and devotion.'

She concluded in terms of fervent affection.

The captain kissed the letter, and read it twice, and whilst he was putting it in his pocket with the care of a document worth thousands, he was hailed from the quay alongside.

' How d'ye, Jackman ?'

He looked over and saw a middle-aged man dressed in the pilot cloth of the master's wear.

' How are you, Phillips ?'

' Any good news for me in that letter you've just now pocketed ?'

Jackman made no reply.

' Got a ship yet ?'

The other flourished his hand over his brig.

'Ah, but that's the monkey eating his own tail.' After a pause—'Has any further news,' cried the captain on the quay, 'been heard of the money you were robbed of?'

'It's long ago washed down fifteen hundred throats, and purchased enjoyment of fifteen hundred hideous revelries,' answered Jackman, nodding and smiling; and saying this, he passed forward, and the captain ashore walked on, with a single turn of his head to gaze at the ship, as if considering Jackman's business in fitting her out and how much the job cost.

Jackman was a master in expression of face; had he combined the other necessary qualities he would have been the greatest actor of his day, and risen to the large reputation of Mr. Kemble or Mr. Kean. Nobody but must have imagined that he was vastly tickled by the inquiries about the stolen money sung up by the captain on the quay. His face, having recovered from its smile, wore its ordinary placid and even sweet expression, and with that face upon him he conversed about the affairs of the brig with the man who had touched his hat to him on his entering the vessel. He did not carry the dramatic airs of the sailor; that generation of seamen were leaving those airs for the American boasters to import. He looked a thorough gentleman, dressed indeed with some reference to his vocation, but as one who does not love to represent himself a sailor by his clothes.

He roamed a little while about his brig, and spoke a friendly word here and there to some of the men.

This brig would be laughed at in this age as a heavy old waggon, and so she showed as she sat upon the water, because of her very square stern, her breadth of beam, and the very preposterous steeve which they gave to their bowsprits in the beginning of this age. Yet, carrying lofty masts, and being very square-rigged, she did not show as the stumpy bulk which she looked when you gazed forward from her taffrail. Her lines at her cutwater, running well aft, might have been laid in Aberdeen, and, though she was plump aft, they had given her a lift of counter which raised her after-part clear of that drawing roll of sea, which plump

ships of this sort are in the habit of dragging
with them. On deck she was simply
equipped as a trading brig should be. She
had a little green caboose for cooking the
men's dinner in ; a forecastle under deck,
with a square hole to enter by, painted casks
for liquor and meat ; skylights aft, and a
plain companion conducting to the cabin.

Such was the brig *Gypsy*, 180 tons, Jackman commander, bequeathed to him by his
father, who had also received her as a bequest
from *his* father.

He lingered on board the greater part
of the day, superintending the business of
fitting out, but in a furtive sort of way,
almost noticeable to any one with sharp
sight, as though, in fact, he did not belong
to the brig. He went ashore at five o'clock,
walking slowly, and carefully reading his
sweetheart's letter.

A journey by coach to anywhere, in the
time of this book, was an achievement more
or less significant. Men made their wills
before their departure. They were in the
right. What are the risks of the rail as
compared with the risks of the road ? You

have the collision.   In the good old times
you had the masked highwayman with the
loaded pistols, and the horrible threat ; you
had the deep ditch into which the great
lumbering coach, in some transport of
downhill manœuvring, was overset.   You
had lanes of mud, in which all got out and
shoved ; you had the dangers of long
exposure to the air, so that when you
finally arrived you were nearly dead with
some affection of the chest.

Some hundreds of miles away from
London, measurable now in a day by
steam, in those times in about a week,
stood a little village of the hard Cornwall
grey stone that makes Penzance, in spite
of its architecture, picturesque.   The village
was on the coast, distant about two miles
from the sea, and was pretty with many
little gardens, and remarkable in its air of
genial originality ; as though, having grown
so far afield, it had borrowed its prejudices
nowhere.   A village inn fronted the high
road.   It swung the sign of 'Nelson.'   Nelson
was still much in the public mind in those
days.   A stoutly built fellow in a lazy,

lounging walk, came to the door, and,
looking up the road, said to some one
within—

'What makes the coach late?'

'They time themselves out o' greediness,
and can't keep their word!' exclaimed a
female voice.

Now, as this was said, a noise of distant
thunder was heard, and lo! the coach, at
hard gallop, turned the corner, the guard
bugling, and the foam flaking from the
horses' mouths. It rattled up, with all the
fine effect of those glistening, grandly
handled vehicles, to the door of the
'Nelson,' and stopped, the horses blowing
smoke, and one white female face, prim
in a Quaker's bonnet, staring through an
inside window.

There was a single traveller on top of
the coach. He had his cloak rolled well
around him, and descended with the movements of a half-frozen man. He asked for
something to eat and drink, and was shown
into a parlour where, with as little loss of
time as possible, they served him handsomely
with chops and potatoes and excellent beer.

He then produced a pipe, and sat with his feet to the fire. On the entrance of the landlord to remove the dishes, Captain Jackman said languidly—

'Can I have a bed in your house?'

'Yes, sir.'

'I am here to visit a man named Thomas Bruton. Do you know him?'

'Well, I've known Tom half my life.'

'Do you think he would come across and talk with me on a business matter I have in mind?'

'I'll fetch him for you now, sir. If he's out, he can't be far off. He lives but five doors down.'

The landlord went out with a load of plates and dishes, and Captain Jackman sat musing in front of the fire, of whose warmth and comfort he was greatly in need. After a short absence the landlord returned, accompanied by a man whose extremely ugly face discovered many marks of astonishment. He bobbed from side to side to catch a view of the gentleman who wanted him. He wore a little grey wig, and was deeply pitted with small-pox; he was blind of one eye, and the other looked into his nose, so that it amazed those he conversed with that he saw them.

'Is it Thomas Bruton that you want, gentleman?' said the man, stepping round the table to the side of the captain and staring at him.

'Are you he?' answered Jackman, rising and smiling.

'Ay, and not ashamed of it,' responded the fellow, whose appearance was decidedly villainous.

'I want ten minutes' talk with you; sit down. Landlord, fetch this gentleman a pint of ale, and kindly leave us.'

This was done. Bruton continued to run his malevolent eye with amazement all over the captain, who resumed his seat.

'I understand,' began Captain Jackman, 'that you are the proprietor of a little property, some twelve or fifteen miles down the coast here, called Bugsby's Hole.'

'They're right who says so,' answered the man, sitting squarely before his liquor.

'You want to sell it?'

'To him as 'll buy, yes.'

' First, what's your price ?'

' Sixty pound cash down. I've lived in that house myself, and can warrant it.'

' I'll give you that money for it, if the house and the neighbourhood and the cave suit me,' said Jackman.

' You want the cave too !' said the man, with an ugly expressive grin.

' I buy the house because I may require the cave.'

' Well,' said the man after a little reflection, ' ye shall have the cave in.   First class of their sort they are ; but they never would ha' been included if ye hadn't offered for the house outright, nor would I ha' been willin' to let the house on any terms.'

' So I had gathered, and was prepared for.   Ask no questions,' said the captain, ' and I'll ask none.   When can I view the property ?'

Bruton pulled out a heavy gold watch.

' Not to-day !' exclaimed the captain, ' I am dog-tired.   Can you procure a vehicle so that we may start to-morrow at about ten o'clock ?'

'Right, sir!' said the man with a great manner of cheerfulness.

At the hour named Bruton drove up to the 'Nelson Inn' in a light cart drawn by a small strong horse, and Captain Jackman got in. A little crowd had collected to witness their going. A stranger was the rarest of coast gulls in those parts. His face, his apparel, his bearing, suggested a distant place and another sort of civilization. Bruton flicked his horse, and they started down a pebbly roaring road. There was no talking. They went over ruts and ridges presently at a rate of about ten miles an hour, and the captain was flung over Bruton's knee, and still there was no talking.

At last they came to a level plain of moor, sallow, discoloured, desolate as the edge of coast and rim of sea that was now sweeping round to their progress so as to meet them. Then the captain could make Bruton hear this—

'Do you ever use your house for the running of goods?'

'Who are you that I should report

myself ?' And the squint turned fiercely upon Jackman.

'Oh, I can be candid with such as you,' exclaimed the captain, with a loud laugh. '*You* don't peach. You have secrets which keep you men of honour. See here, now.' He laid his hand upon Bruton's shoulder, and said, 'I am pirate and smuggler !'

'Where have you been running ?'

'Folkestone.'

'Ye h'ant got the looks of one of us.'

'I am a gentleman,' exclaimed Jackman warmly, 'with as determined a resolution to make a fortune as others have. The sea promises a good yield. You must have done well out of her to live without work at your time of life.'

'The ocean's paid me well. I'm bound to say that,' said Mr. Bruton, relaxing. 'And since you're so free, so'll I be. The cottage and the cave I'm a-driving you to, and which'll soon heave in sight, was used by me and my missis and the children as a dwelling-house and a storeroom for the choicest of the run goods, the rest being stowed in secret places, or in the steps.'

' The steps,' echoed the captain.

'Ay, you can step down to the foam of
the water.   It's a low front of cliff here-
abouts.'

' Were you successful in your hidings ?'

' To tell you the truth,' the man answered in a grumbling note of laughter,
' we were so rarely troubled that I believe
we came off with nigh everything we got
ashore.'

' Piracy is a dangerous trade,' said Captain Jackman, talking to this man as if he
was a brother pirate.   'My ship is not to be
seen once too often in that market, and
newly rigged and freshly painted, she may
complete the sum of money I want, and
which as a gentleman I cannot possibly live
without, if we rig her afresh and paint her a
new colour.'

Bruton turned his squint eye upon his
companion.   He scarcely knew what to
think of him.   ' Where's your gang ?' said
he.

' I have men fit to board and capture a
line-of-battle ship,' was the answer.

Bruton pointed dumbly ahead with his

whip; and Jackman saw a little cottage upon
the horizon, the most melancholy picture in
the world under the grey sky, and set to the
music of the wind that was now coming a
little wildly off that opening eye of sea on
their left. They drove rapidly, and drew up
at the cottage door. It was a strong house,
fit for a powder-magazine, built of Cornish
flag, put together with a heedlessness of
aspect that lent it beauty of the roughest
sort.

It had several little windows on either
side, a fair piece of ground plotted out at
the back, a small front garden, and was
certainly a dead broke bargain with its
stairs, even for moral living, at the money
asked.

Bruton made his horse fast, pulled out a
key, and they entered his singular, very
much detached house. It was dusty and
grimy, and showed a great plenty of beer
stains, and rum stains, and perhaps blood
stains. It was naked to the windows of
furniture. It stood waiting for the hurricanes
of that iron coast to beat it down and lay its
spirit to soil.

'This will do,' said Jackman, after looking over the house. 'Show me your stairs, Mr. Bruton.'

But first Mr. Bruton exposed a number of secret hiding-places in the house itself, the sight of which greatly delighted Captain Jackman. They were perfect, he thought, as places of concealment. They next went to the stairs. These were entered from without. They had no trap or cover.

'What's the good of a hatch?' said Mr. Bruton, descending.

The sea-flash in the base gave them light, and the light behind followed them. Mr. Bruton pointed to one or two avenues in which he said Captain Jackman and his hearties would find hiding-places — none more perfect along the coast, all open now, and so discoverable, being no longer needed. They stood on a step clear of the massive belch of the breaker.

'There's some fine weather here for landing, I suppose?'

'If there wasn't,' said Mr. Bruton, 'how should I be now worth my fourteen thousand pounds, two 'ouses, not counting this one,

and a comfortable lugger for my diversion, if
I hadn't snicked it all off the revenue ?'

'Good, come up,' cried Captain Jackman,
with excitement. 'Let your gains be mine,
and I'll bless your name.'

'Will you buy the house ?' said the man.

'Yes,' answered the captain, 'and return
with you to the town, where you'll recom-
mend me to people who'll clean and furnish
it comfortably whilst I am away on business
elsewhere.'

'That shall be done, sir, and under my
superintendence,' said Bruton, as they
emerged, followed by the distant hollow
roar of the sea.

*   *   *   *   *

Commander Conway strode impatiently
about his little parlour. It was breakfast
time, and there was a smell of fried fish in
the house. Putting his head out he caught
sight of Mrs. Dove at the end of the passage,
and cried—

'Why does Miss Ada keep me waiting ?
Go and let her know that breakfast is
ready, and tell her to come down, dressed or
undressed.'

He was warm with temper, and wiped his face. His daughter had for years been a mortification to him in a quiet way. She would snub him in company, she would decline to walk with him. She was for ever expressing detestation of the place, knowing that her father, in stern reality, could not afford a move. In the depths of his soul, the old gentleman felt a little sick of these yearly experiences of his, and was perfectly willing to marry her to any one whom he should think fit to be her husband. Jackman was not that man. What was there in that man that made the austere, keen-eyed commander witness a character in his beauty invisible to the girl ? Conway had mixed with men, and knew human nature. Of one dark side of man's character or spirit he could claim a particular knowledge.

These thoughts ran in his head whilst he waited. Suddenly he heard Mrs. Dove, who was a very slow woman, come tumbling downstairs, and in a moment she had fallen against Conway.

' What now ?' said the commander, sternly thrusting her back.

'As I live to say it, sir,' cried the poor old
lady, in broken tones of purest agitation and
fright, 'Miss Ada didn't sleep under your
roof last night !'

The enraged commander studied the old
working face with a gaze horrible with
menace, then thrusting past her he went
upstairs and entered his daughter's room.
The bed had been untouched. Certainly
she had said 'Good-night' to him on the
landing. She had left when the house was
in darkness, suppose an hour after saying
'Good-night.'   With whom had she eloped ?
Most undoubtedly with that scoundrel,
Captain Jackman.

The commander stood in the middle of
his daughter's room, looking round him.
His strong breast hove a sob once, and he
muttered to himself, 'What shall I do ?'
The runaway had ten hours' advantage of
any pursuit; but whither, to what place
should she be pursued ? Had she left no
note, no communication ?   But then,
although she had not slept in her bed, *had*
she eloped ? The commander went downstairs to eat his breakfast.

Mrs. Dove stood in the room, white with anxiety and agitation.

'Oh, commander, is she gone, do you think? Is she gone off, do you imagine, with the sea captain?' And she wrung her hands, and her face worked in wrinkles.

'With whom else?' sternly replied the commander, seating himself before his favourite fried sole, and beginning a breakfast that scarcely promised its usual heartiness.

'What can be done, sir, to save her?'

'Don't you know, ma'm,' answered the commander, 'it has been said, that the virtue that needs a sentinel is not worth guarding? What would *you* do to save her? She's ahead of us by ten or eleven hours. The heart of ice had no damned right to leave me without a single farewell or word of her intention.'

'I can't believe that, sir. I *can't* believe she'd go off without leaving a note. I'll make another search.'

She stumped upstairs. The commander ate his fish, often looking hard out of the window. Keen distress worked in his bosom.

But his face of iron masked it.   She had left no letter, he thought to himself.   *She* would have no talent at kindness in unkindness. She must sheath her knife to the hilt to make the stroke effectual to her.   As he thought thus, Mrs. Dove entered bearing a note.   Her face had lost its working wrinkles of horror ; she entered with something of gaiety.

'I've found this behind the dressing-table, where it had been blown down by the draught from the open window.   I knew— I knew, dear heart, she wouldn't go away without saying good-bye.'

She handed the letter to the commander, who quietly put down his knife and fork, took the letter, and read—

'Commander Conway, R.N.'

He then opened the letter.   It was of two folded sheets, with very little in them, and the missive ran thus—

'DEAR FATHER,

'I am eloping to-night with my darling Walter Jackman.   This uncomfortable form of marriage need not have hap-

pened had you proved reasonable, but you
were ever in extremes in your likes and dislikes. I am now going to be happy after
many years of dulness and contemptible
vexations, where my beauty was fast yellow-
ing, and where I had not a friend whom I
valued. I do not say where we are going,
for I do not want you to give yourself the
trouble of following me. It is impossible
for you to miss me. We saw so little of
each other. It was only the sense of my
being in the house that gave you satisfaction.
I will write to you when I am settled,
and shall hope to hear from you. And
so, with love, and a kiss of farewell, and
begging you will not take this too much to
heart,

'I am,

'Your always affectionate daughter,

'ADA CONWAY.'

'Always affectionate daughter!' rasped
out the commander, bringing his fist down
on a sheet of the letter. 'How do you
like the notion of calling Ada Conway
Mrs. Walter Jackman?'

And he ground his teeth, and left the breakfast-table.

'I am glad I found the letter,' said Mrs. Dove. 'It shows she's not so bad. But, oh, she's wicked—she's wicked to treat her poor old father so.'

Conway cut the old woman short by stepping on to his lawn. He filled a pipe, and paced to and fro. A little cannon stood at each corner of this lawn, and amidships there had been reared a mighty flagstaff, which one night came down in a gale of wind with an incredible thunder of noise. It did little mischief; yet had it struck the commander's house, it is odds, seeing that his bedroom immediately faced it, if it had not smashed him as flat as his roof.

He walked for some time meditating in exasperation. He was helpless. What could he do? Presently there came along the cliff's side, within easy hail of the commander, Mr. Leaddropper and Captain Burgoyne. Both men were wrapped in stout pilot-cloth, and the sea never shaped, chiselled, coloured, clothed, and sent adrift to get a living a more perfect sailor than Burgoyne.

They saw Conway, and came rolling across.

' Sorry to hear the bad news, commander,' said Leaddropper.

Conway stared. ' How the devil should you know it ?' he roared. ' It's scarcely known to myself yet !'

' We met the butcher, who had called for orders,' said Burgoyne. ' You'll never get a servant to keep a secret. And it's nigh halfway over the town already.'

' Commander,' exclaimed old Leaddropper in a broken voice, ' I am truly sorry for you.'

' A plague on all sorrow !' burst out Conway, breathing short.

' But it's the business of all parents to get their daughters married,' continued the pilot; ' and you weren't going to find soundings for her in that way here. She's done for herself; and since she's done it, why,' cried he, with a rollicking air, ' let us take the earliest occasion to drink their healths !'

' Leaddropper,' said Burgoyne, who saw

that Conway could scarcely contain his
rage, ' I don't think the commander rightly
relishes this talk just now.   Can I be of
any service to you ?' he exclaimed, frankly
addressing Conway.

' Thanks.   I am an old man, and this
blow has somewhat stunned me.   She was
my only child, and I am a widower.   I
should wish for prudent counsel.   Although
they be married, I should like to know
whether she's not to be torn from the
beggar's embraces, and brought back here
and locked up clear of him.'

His companions gravely shook their
heads.

' Have you any idea where she's gone
to ?' asked the pilot.

' To sea in the beggar's brig ; that's my
opinion.'

' So he's got a brig,' said the pilot,
interested.   ' He may turn out better than
you think.'

They discoursed for some time in this
style.   They were all equally ignorant, and
had therefore nothing to suggest or communicate.   This idle council concluded by

the commander swearing that he would go to London by next day's coach, visit the owners of the *Lovelace*, and make all human and possible inquiries in the docks about the man Jackman, his brig, his antecedents ; and, for all he knew, he might in this way get to find out where his daughter was; for the scoundrel Jackman was pretty certain to make sail for London, where his brig was, and where also he could easily get married.

It was a tremendous undertaking—very expensive, very cold at that time of the year, tedious beyond any words in human speech, and it was now twelve years since the commander had visited the Metropolis on top of a West of England mail-coach. Behold him next day seated on the roof of a stout, handsome, well-apparelled vehicle ! On his arrival in London he was nearly dead, in spite of the several comfortable breaks. He had long been used to his own armchair and his own bed, and hated travelling by coach. Nevertheless, here he was at last in that marvellous Metropolis, which staggers the nose more than any other sense on one's first entry on top of a vehicle from miles of turnips and acres of grain.

It was twelve o'clock in the day. The commander descended stiff from the coach, entered a neighbouring eating-house, where he called for a plate of beef and a pint of ale, which did him good. He then, after making full inquiry, walked to the offices of the owners of the ship *Lovelace*. Only one of her owners was at business. This was the tall, rather gentlemanly man, Sir William Williams, who bent his body in halves when he talked, and preserved most of the styles of the last age. On his learning that the tall gentleman was an owner, the commander told him who he was, and begged for an interview. This was immediately granted, and they repaired together to a small back office, bulk-headed off by glass panels.

'I have travelled many leagues, sir,' began the commander, 'to obtain at this office any information that may enable me to get at one Captain Jackman, who, I bitterly lament to say, after haunting our

parts, has,' he continued, colouring with
emotion and shame, 'run away with my
daughter, my only child.'

Sir William looked at him gravely and
sympathetically. 'I will not go behind
anything your feelings may dictate,' he
said. 'We hold our own opinion of the
fellow at this office. I do not think it's
likely that he will find employment under
any other house-flag, let alone ours. His
name has become notorious through his loss
of the fifteen hundred sovereigns belonging
to us.'

'It was no more stolen from him——'
began the commander.

Sir William lifted his hand, with a grave
smile. 'We know that he has been spend-
ing money in your parts,' he said; 'but,
then, he may tell you that that is the money
with which we paid him off. He has
equipped his brig. He will prove to you
that he has borrowed money upon her for
trading purposes. Unless he may be con-
victed, we would rather not touch him.
Proofs to the hilt, or silence, that is my
theory of our British law.'

'Has he been seen about the docks?' asked the commander.

'I don't know.'

'He is fitting out his brig, isn't he?'

'She sailed some days ago.'

'Where bound to?'

'Nominally to Oporto,' answered Sir William, smiling.

'*He* could not have been in charge. The fellow has only a few hours' start of me.'

'They may have come up to London to be married, and they may join the brig after they're man and wife,' said Sir William, viewing the commander's face with concern.

'Then she'll be hove to, waiting for them!' cried Conway. 'Surely she'd be in the river! By Heaven, I may intercept them yet, and give him hell, if nothing worse happens!'

Sir William, who lived very strictly after the fashion of most shipowners, looked very grave for a moment; then, unbending, he said—

'Your ear, sir.' And after whispering he sprang erect.

And the commander shouted, 'I had

suspected it from the moment of my
setting eyes on him ! The brig must be
in the river ! They'll join her leisurely !
She'll want to see the sights ! I'll intercept
her ! But they will be married—they will
be married !'

Sir William accompanied him to the
pavement, and promised him all the information he could obtain, both as to the man
and as to the brig.

CHAPTER VI.

FATHER AND DAUGHTER.

THE brig *Gypsy* lay in the Thames off Grave-send. She had been fast at her mooring buoy for some days. She was now fully equipped for the sea, and a very handsome boat, pierced for three guns of a side, with place for a pivoted long nine-pounder forward or aft.

In those days the peaceful trader often sailed from the Thames with guns run out. Especially did she need to give this hint if her course for traffic carried her into the ways where the galley-pirate still lingered, where the slave-ship troubled the waters with her hellish keel, where, in short, there were numerous vessels afloat of very doubt-ful respectability.

Here, then, lay the brig *Gypsy*, Captain

Jackman's heirloom, and much good had his worthy father hoped it would do him. Men in craft, pushing slowly by in bows as round as a potato, gazed at the brig with admiration. They would like to have such a little vessel to command. She was going to make a pleasant voyage, bet your heart. She certainly looked more like a pleasure craft rigged as a sham trader, than a vessel of commerce, and many would have expected to see the dresses of ladies fluttering on board of her, and a number of gentlemen, well dressed, ready for the start, and for enjoyment.

It was the fifth day of the *Gypsy's* detention. The river was running rapidly and bearing all sorts of vessels seawards, whilst those forging inwards had to strike with a forefoot of claws to catch the way the breeze was giving them. It was a dull afternoon. The shipping showed shabbily. The water flowed in lead, and the sky was a rainy brown, sickly with the slow motion of unwholesome yellow cloud. A large man, with a huge face made up as it might appear of pieces of putty, the seams showing so as to render his mask of face extraordinary, overhung the bulwark rail, with his foot on a carronade, and his gaze bent on a boat that was approaching the brig almost athwart stream from the Gravesend pier. The wrinkles grew deep in his brow as the boat neared the vessel, until, giving a wild laugh, he cried to himself, ' Blow'd if it ain't Commander Conway !'

The men got their boat alongside, and the commander handed himself up the three or four steps which lay over the gangway. The huge putty-faced man saluted him.

' I thought you'd know me, Hoey. Are they aboard ?'

' You mean the master and wife, sir ?'

' No one else,' said the commander.

' They are not, then, and we've been here fooling around this buoy five days.'

' You're mate of this ship, aren't you ?' said the commander.

' Yes, sir,' answered the man, with something of a lumpish grin.

' How many mates have you ?'

' Myself and another.'

' I mean to remain on board until the

arrival of my daughter, and then,' said the commander firmly, almost to grimness, 'shall ask you, Bill Hoey, to set me and her ashore at our home, which is a good way down Channel, as of course you know.'

'I've signed articles under Captain Jackman. I can take no liberties, I am afraid.'

'We shall see. I will bring you and the others to a right state of mind before I've done with you,' said the commander, shooting sharp glances in the direction of a number of seamen who were lounging on the forecastle and smoking, and looking at the land, and apparently filling their end of the little ship with their numbers.

'Can you give us any idea when the captain's coming off, sir?' said Hoey.

'He may be here to-day, or to-morrow, or next day. He'll not long tarry. I have hunted the docks for good purpose, and have gathered information which I shall communicate to the crew in proper time. Where are you bound to, do you think?'

The huge Bill Hoey made no answer, and looked sheepish.

11

'You are cleared for the port of Oporto,' continued the commander.

'For the land of romance, more likely,' answered Bill Hoey, who, laughing respectfully, saluted and crossed the deck, his dutifulness—which is one of the glories of the English seaman—being alarmed by the commander's questions and his unrevealed knowledge.

The commander went to the side, paid the boatmen, received his valise, dismissed the boat, and seeing a man approaching the little companion, he gave him the valise and told him to take it below.

'Into the living room, sir ?' said the man.

'Death and fire, has it come to a sailor not knowing what below means !'

'But what's your cabin ?' said the fellow sulkily; 'that's what I meant. There are but three ; two's occupied, and one's the pantry.'

'Take that thing below !' repeated the commander, gesticulating with a shovel-shaped hand, and speaking in that tone of voice to which the blue-jacket is used when the naval officer's digestion is a little out of repair. The commander then made the rounds of the brig. He gazed first with astonishment and attention at the guns, the tompions of which were in. He studied the little brig aloft, and secretly admired her.

'What a villain,' he said to himself, 'to marry my daughter, and then put his ship to this use !'

'I beg your pardon, sir,' said Hoey the mate, coming over to him, 'but is your honour sailing with us ?'

'I am just doing what I blessed well please,' cried the commander, blood-red with rage at being questioned by a man filling Hoey's post. 'You will do me the favour to leave me alone, merely sending the steward to me, as I am going below.'

The habit of command was to be seen in the commander. Hoey read the taut discipline of the quarter-deck in old Conway, from his white hair to his buckled shoes. He touched his cap, as though the commander had been the skipper himself. Conway went below, and in a few minutes a young seaman, dressed in a camlet jacket, made his appearance. Conway had been looking round the cabin. It was a com-

fortable little berth. A table equal to
dining two persons at a time was fixed
amidship, and there were three sleeping
berths, one of which was the pantry and
larder.

'I shall want to sleep here,' said the
commander. 'That's my valise. Where
can I rest my head o' night down Channel?'

The young steward, recognising something very superior to the average officer
he was used to, in this square man of
fighting aspect, said—

'The capt'n sleeps there, and his lady
there, sir. And this 'ere's been made a
pantry of,' and he opened the little door.

There was an unnecessary variety of
crockery, all of a much too expensive sort
for a common little trading brig. The
commander stood wrapped in contemplation.
He then looked at a locker which ran along
the ship's side parallel with the table, and
formed, so to speak, a bench.

'That'll make me all the bed I want,'
said he. 'Which is my daughter's berth?'

'The starboard one, sir.'

The commander walked into it, followed

like a sentry by the steward, who could not understand this severe square gentleman's cool procedure on board a ship that did not belong to him.

Conway saw a little trunk belonging to his daughter. A handbag was hanging under a looking-glass. Under the glass was a small oil-painting of Captain Walter Jackman, stiff in high coat collars, his gift to his love. The rest consisted of the ordinary fittings of a bunk to sleep in, of a little wash-stand, and so forth.

The commander, taking no notice of the steward, walked on deck. He was warmly clad in thick pilot. He made for the weather quarter-deck at once, and Mr. Hoey, seeing him coming, edged forward, and trudged in the waist with askant looks aft. It was something after two. The stream of tide was slacking. The houses of Gravesend were faintly discernible through a delicate drizzle of squall that was just then blowing over them. The cold and melancholy waste, where now stand the civilising signs of great docks and tall masts, made the scene that way soul depressing.

Hard by the fort lay a little cutter of sixty or seventy tons. The pennant of the state flickered at her mast-head, and Commander Conway frequently directed his attention at the little craft as he stumped his few feet of deck.

Nobody seemed to notice that Conway usurped the quarter-deck. In fact, it had been breezed abroad that he was the father-in-law of the master of the brig, and Jack was therefore satisfied. For an hour or so things remained as they were : Gravesend hung in squall ; Tilbury ran off its banks in gleams of mud ; the little cutter, with her gaff mainsail hoisted, strained at her cable ; and all between were great ships and little ships coming and going. Those who came were bound to London town, and those who went were being steered down the noble stream to every port in the world.

An hour after Commander Conway had arrived on board the *Gypsy*, a wherry might have been seen putting off with feathering blade and smart whip of oar in the direction of the brig.

' Here they come !' said the commander ;

and he knocked the ashes of his pipe over the rail.

The boat rapidly glanced athwart the tide; the commander continued to strut to and fro. Hoey stood at the open gangway ready to receive the party. The boat hooked on, and swarmed through the rush of waters abreast to alongside. Captain and Mrs. Jackman stepped on board. The boat put off, and Hoey, turning to the commander, shouted—

'Are you going ashore, sir?'

'Yes, and with my daughter,' said the commander, advancing towards Ada, who slightly shrank.

'Pray, sir, what business have you in this vessel?' demanded Captain Jackman with a very dark face.

'My business is that lady whom you have feloniously removed from my roof, and now intend to carry into some sort of calling— smuggling, they call it—which may wholly ruin her.'

'Nonsense!' exclaimed the young lady. 'What I did was done entirely of my own free will, and I will do it again. He is my husband. You cannot separate us ; you cannot take me ashore because you wish to see us sundered.'

She stood all her inches as she said these words, and spoke with her full strength of voice, and the sailors listened eagerly. Reckoned on the whole, she was the finest girl out of the port of London.

' Weigh anchor !' shouted Captain Jackman to Hoey, whose voice instantly went forward in the proper cow-like roar.

It was an old-fashioned capstan, and it was worked with a song, and there were thirty throats. By degrees those looking over the rail saw the shore slipping by and inward-bound vessels coming along fast. Sail floated to the masthead, and blew balloon-like at the topgallant mast. Captain Jackman, after speaking a word with his wife, crossed the deck, where Conway stepped, the picture of violated law, indignant father, and horror of the whole proceedings.

' Is it your intention, sir, to make this cruise with us ? If so, you are very welcome ; another nautical sabreur will please me vastly.'

'You are carrying me away at your own risk. You have stolen my daughter. I mean that you shall set me ashore, and I intend that my daughter shall accompany me home.'

'To what home?' cried Jackman.

'To the home you stole her from!' shouted Conway.

'She has a home of her own!' exclaimed Captain Jackman, drawing himself up with the gravity and dignity of an earl who talks of a belt and acres. 'As you are accompanying us, you shall visit us in that home, and judge if your daughter is not perfectly comfortable.'

With that he turned scornfully on his heel, and crossed the deck to speak to Mrs. Jackman.

Meanwhile, those who noticed anything had observed that the cutter lying in shore had loosed her mainsail and was getting her anchor. The evening gathered. The cutter was manifestly giving chase. The brig floated in lofty and silent contempt through the wide reaches. At seven o'clock the captain, followed by Ada, came out of the cabin, and found the commander pacing the deck smoking a pipe. Captain Jackman, slightly raising his hat, went up to him, and said—

' Since, sir, you are deliberately a guest of the brig's, you will allow me to force her hospitality upon you.'

' Oh, presently ! A biscuit, that will do, thank you,' answered the commander, in his gruffest notes. ' I am an old sailor.'

The captain, making no answer, crossed into the gloom, where, he perceived, stood the burly shape of Bill Hoey.

' Summon all hands aft; I have something to say to them,' said he, and then rejoined his wife, who had remained silently watching her father pacing the deck, and trying in vain to imagine what he intended to do.

There came aft, on the quarter-deck, a large number of men for so small a craft, despite that vessels went very liberally handled in those days. They filled the waist and all about the mainmast ; and the commander, poising his pipe at his mouth, stood watching them in something of a posture of astonish-

ment.   The dusk rendered faces and figures
imperfect.   It might be seen, however, that,
in addition to her batteries of guns, and stern
and bow chasers, she carried a crew as powerful almost as a man-of-war of small rating
would have entered.

Captain Jackman, leaving his wife's side,
stepped in front of the men, and said, in a
high note of exultation—

'Men, I have called you aft not to make
you a speech, but to give you two or three
facts, all of which I know will warm you to
the very roots of your souls.   I told you, for
purposes of signing, that I had pretended we
were bound to the Portugal coast, but that,
in reality, we were bound away in search of
a treasure, the particulars of which I gave
you.   That was a lie.   We are no treasure-
seekers, unless it lie in the holds of others.
Men,' he cried, now beginning to gesticulate,
and to warm up with his fancies, 'this beautiful little brig has been fitted up as a pirate'
—the commander's pipe dropped with his
hand—' and a smuggler,' continued Jackman.
'I have a date for a ship sailing from Lisbon.
She will make your fortune; and I swear

you will go in no risk.　That is what I have
to say to you, men.　Turn it over, and consider how magnificently it must work, seeing
that in the south of Cornwall I already
possess a splendid estate of smuggling steps
and caves, and a little house in which my
wife will live till we have completed our
business, in which time Commander Conway
may be glad to prove one of the party.　He
will be welcome.'

A curious murmur rose from amongst the
crew.　No man could clearly catch the exact
word or groan.

The cutter astern was leaning over to
the damp evening blast, which was now
beginning to breeze up ; and her wake
went astern of her as though it was the
shimmer of her canvas.

'Bear a hand in making sail, Mr. Hoey,'
shouted Jackman ; and the great fellow
answered with a roar, and the sailors sprang
about.

Swift as was the brig, however, the cutter
proved a swifter keel, and by half-past ten
o'clock that night she had ranged within
easy hail of the *Gypsy*.

' Brig ahoy !' came a loud voice through the moist dissembling gloom. ' What ship are you, and where are you bound to ?'

' We are the brig *Gypsy*, of and from London, and bound to the coast of Portugal,' answered Captain Jackman, who had sprung on the rail of his vessel when the other had hailed him.

The commander rushed to the ship's side. ' Nothing of the sort, sir. He's no honest ship ; he's going for a pirate and a smuggler. I am Commander——'

He had shouted this in a voice like a speaking trumpet, when Captain Jackman rounded upon him, fiercely levelling a pistol at his head as he did so.

' Down, you old dog !' he cried, stepping close to Conway. ' Speak another word, and even your daughter's presence sha'n't save your life ! Go below, sir, so as to be out of danger ! Below, sir !—below, sir, I say !' This he said, thrusting him towards the companion way.

' I'll square the yards yet with you, you scoundrel !' exclaimed the commander ; and with a lingering look at the cutter, that was whitening the gloom with foam and canvas to windward, he vanished.

Shortly after he had descended into the cabin, his daughter arrived. A bright lamp was swinging; the remains of supper were upon the table. The girl looked fiercely under her black crooked brows at her father, and said, in a voice of hot contempt—

'What right have you on board this ship?'

'The right of a father,' shouted the commander, 'to fetch his daughter away from a pirate and a smuggler.'

'You cannot separate us,' she cried.

'You shall go ashore with me, or I shall stick to this ship,' he answered.

She arched her mouth into a sneer, and said, 'I would advise you to leave us to our fate. You are never likely to hear of us; and your reputation, of which you think highly, will be safe. If you interfere—— But, as it is, you have already given the news to the revenue cutter on our quarter, even whilst our own sailors may be considering whether they shall sail in the ship or not.'

As she spoke these words, there was a

sharp hail abeam, quite audible in the cabin. It was not answered from the brig, which was now sheeting through the sea under tall leaning heights, beating the water into sifted snow with the drive of her round bows. The hail was repeated. A minute later the *Gypsy* was fired at; the glare of the gun illuminated the little cabin port-hole. The shot made the old hull thrill, and she broke off somewhat wildly to a sudden frightened whirl of smoke. The commander, fully expecting that Captain Jackman would heave-to, rushed on deck just in time to behold some men abaft the wheel of the *Gypsy* bringing a nine-pounder to bear upon the little foaming hull. As he rushed to the side, the gun was fired. A sharp sound of crackling followed, and, more to the consternation than the gratification, perhaps, of the brig's company, they beheld the fabric of mainmast cut sheer in halves by the shot, and the whole litter and smother of gear and canvas encumbering the deck. She came to a stand. The *Gypsy* sped on.

'Do you know what you have done, sir?' cried the commander.

'I have served him as I intend to serve others,' was the answer. 'You stand in my way. I am an honest man; this is a clean ship. What law can justify that scoundrel in firing at me?'

'Your refusal to answer the hail of a king's ship. What are you bringing yourself into?' And with something frantic in his manner, the old fellow went in long strides to the stern of the vessel.

He stood watching the cutter sending up signals. They might have been colours of danger, hurried flashes of distress. No notice was taken on board the brig—in fact, the crew seemed all too much afraid of what had happened to be willing to stop the *Gypsy*, even had the order to back her topsail been given. A king's cutter hulled, dismasted, placed *hors de combat* by an English brig which had impudently refused to heave-to to legitimate demands! Who was this Captain Jackman, anyhow? It had got mysteriously whispered about, through God knows what source, that he was a little mad. It may have come from his last ship. It may have been detected in the docks, and coolly noted and made nothing of by the reckless seamen who had agreed to sail with him for fine pay and a good share of the treasure.

The wide stretch of river looked melancholy with the black of the night and the dimness of the stars, and the dull gleam of the heads of the running sea. The commander, with folded arms, stood gazing in the direction where the cutter was sunk in the gloom. His mind was distracted. He had counted upon the civility and respect of Captain Jackman; on the contrary, his life had been threatened, and he was now being carried away to sea in spite of his protests. He could endure his reverie no longer, and after looking about him in search of Captain Jackman, and beholding no one aft but the huge figure of Bill Hoey, who was keeping the watch, he went into the cabin.

There he found the captain and Ada, late as it was, in earnest conversation. They broke off when he entered, and the captain stood up; but the girl stared at her father with angry looks of impatience.

'We are pleased that you have come

below, sir,' said the captain respectfully, indicating a chair, and brandy and other materials, in as many flourishes of his hand. ' We should like a good understanding to exist between us.'

' I am very wishful that that should be,' said the commander, who understood that this lover of good understandings carried loaded pistols in his pockets, and that he had one in his breast then.

' You are on board my brig,' said Captain Jackman, ' without invitation. Do not you think you are guilty of a gross act of rudeness ?'

The commander pointed, mute with passion, to his daughter.

' You cannot divorce us by being here,' continued Captain Jackman, with a slow white smile and a sarcastic face, and eyes full of dangerous light. ' She is my wife, sir, above and beyond your control absolutely.'

' You will set me ashore with her, nevertheless,' exclaimed Commander Conway.

' Yes, you shall be set ashore certainly, and my wife and I will accompany you. Does that satisfy you, sir ?'

'Where is the place?' said the commander, with an angry snuffle of suspicion.

'In Cornwall.'

'It is your home, perhaps.'

'You shall see it,' exclaimed Ada.   'And
when you have enjoyed its beauties you will
return to the little square house.'

The commander looked from one to the
other.   He was very much of an old fool,
but not so foolish as to miss this, that this
couple were not to be dealt with by him,
that he had started on a fool's chase, in which
if he was not very careful with the fellow
opposite, he might lose his life.   He looked
up at the hour that ticked in a clock under
the little hatch.   It was twelve.   He said—

'I will take my rest here, on this locker.'

The captain bowed to him.   'You have
had no refreshment.   May I,' said he, 'offer
you something to eat?'

'I will thank you for a biscuit and a
drop of that brandy.'   He spoke with reluc-
tance, the ill-breeding of which caused his
daughter to fix one of her handsomest
though gloomiest stares upon him.

When the sun rose the brig was standing

down Channel. Sail was heaped on her.
She often foamed to her catheads. She was
making a triumphant course, swift and fine.
The sea about her lay in frosted silver, and
the ships around her leaned in shafts of light.
The commander early made his appearance.
Observing his daughter Ada to be standing
alone at the taffrail, he accosted her.

'Do not you think yourself a very unnatural child ?'

'I am free. Leave me, father, or forbear
at all events from criticising my behaviour,'
answered the girl, flashing her hottest looks
upon him.

'You know that Captain Jackman deliberately stole fifteen hundred pounds of
the moneys of his owners for the purpose
of fitting out his brig for a piratical enter-
prise ?'

'You must prove all that,' she cried.

'He has fired upon a revenue cutter, and
stands to be transported for life.'

'And what then ?' she cried, with a bold
laugh of contempt. 'Wherever he goes he'll
find me near.'

'But you seem to forget that Captain

Jackman, by confessing that he is going as a
pirate, stands to be hanged, and you may see
his corpse on the black mud of the Thames,
revolving at the finger of a gibbet in irons, a
brutally degraded wretch.   My God, what
have you done?'   A great sob rent the old
man's breast.

'Father,' answered the girl, 'I am sorry
to have caused you grief, but my die is cast,
and I beg of you to say no more against my
action, or against my husband.'

She left him and went to the rail, and
watched, with a hot angry face, the white
foam streaming by.   She was absolutely
reckless and defiant.   She had got her man,
and meant to stick to him at all hazards.
The commander walked over to her suddenly,
and putting his arm on her shoulder, exclaimed—

'Do you know that Captain Jackman is
insane?'

'You will have to prove all your statements,' she cried, without turning her head.

'He is a madman,' cried old Conway.   'I
saw it in him when we met.   His owner
told me that he was a madman.   Certain

statements had been made about him by
the crew of his last ship, and in any case
he would not have sailed under their flag
again.'

' Mad or not mad, I love him,' said the
girl, again crossing the deck to avoid her
father.

Meanwhile the crew remained quiet and
obedient. They could not possibly mistake
the ship's errand and the hazard they ran.
Yet they acted as though they had made up
their minds to the consequences. Their
behaviour of obedience greatly puzzled old
Conway, who tried to get at one and another
of them : but somehow they did not choose
to speak. Bill Hoey, in particular, was
peculiarly reticent, considering that he was
plied by a man who had been a Naval Commander, and who carried the authority of the
flag. He would tell nothing, he knew
nothing, he supposed they were going
a-pirating, since the captain said so ; but
who was to tell but that the captain, whose
royal yard did not seemed very well trimmed
by the lifts, might change his mind, go
a-slaving instead, go a-hunting for whales—

in short, the gentleman well knew there was a great deal of business to be done on the seas.

As the brig passed down the coast the commander would from time to time take an eagle view of the starboard horizon, hoping that the cutter had been fallen in with, her case reported, a messenger despatched by land to a port where they had a frigate which would intercept the *Gypsy.* But nothing in the shape of a man-of-war showed the whole way down. They were favoured by fine weather, and in places the sea was white with shafts of canvas. The brig took care to speak nothing. She sailed through the deep without sign, and her secret, whose confession would have brought some of the ships she sighted in fiery pursuit of her, remained her own.

How did the commander fare ? His daughter was not a lovable creature, though a very fine woman. She was not one to sit at table whilst her father walked the deck hungry, nor was the commander one to walk hungry. He said to Captain Jackman—

' I had counted upon you putting me
ashore with my daughter at my home down
the coast, otherwise I should not have
intruded upon you; but since I am here,
I must be fed or die.   Therefore I will
thank you to allow me to join you at your
meals.'

' There has been no intrusion, sir,' said the
captain, in his elegant style.   ' We are glad
to have you with us.   We hope you will
think better of your resolution, and remain
as one who can command us in an expedi-
tion which must result in filling our vaults
with wealth without risk.'   The commander
made an extraordinary face.   ' At all events
I have to go ashore,' exclaimed the captain,
' at Bugsby's Hole with my wife, and we
will take you with us, and perhaps, sir, a
little chat in our quiet home may result in
my scheme gaining your favour.'

The subject then ended, and the commander henceforth fed at the table with his
daughter and son-in-law.   It was an igno-
minious position, and the food nearly choked
the retired officer.   But though he had been
a gallant sailor, he had the usual weaknesses

of the human animal, and amongst these were hunger and thirst.

A day and a night of the bitter weather of the Chops drove the brig to the south'ard under reefed canvas, and some of the sailors wondered if she was going to the Portugal coast, where Jackman had promised them a galleon full of precious commodity. She cleverly regained her place in a couple of days, and on a bright, quiet Sunday morning lay within sight of the part of the Cornwall cliffs which may be here called Bugsby's Hole. The air shone with the white light of winter; the beat of the surf was sullen. This line of coast is low and livid, and its sky-line ran sharp, with not a house or tree to break its dreary continuity. All had been prearranged, and when the brig's maintopsail had been brought to the mast on the ship's arrival at about three-quarters of a mile distant from the land, a large boat was lowered, and a quantity of luggage was put into it. Then Ada entered, next followed the commander, finally the captain, after an earnest conference with Bill Hoey, his chief mate, the man who was to be left in charge.

The boat passed quickly over the long heave of sea which here runs with the weight of the Atlantic, and, watching their opportunity, the men contrived to handsomely beach her within a short walk of Bugsby's Hole. The seamen carried the baggage into the vault, and were followed by the captain, his wife, and the commander. The vault was a fine cutting of a gradual slope, charged on either hand with marvellously contrived hiding-places. They gained the entrance by land, and Captain Jackman was loud in his praise of the beautiful tunnel he had passed through, and which was his property.

' Carry the luggage to that little house yonder,' said Ada. ' That is my home, father. We will convert it into a castle.'

The house that was to be transformed ultimately into a castle, without regard to the laws of the land, and the opinions of respectable seamen sailing the high seas, was an edifice worthy to berth a ploughman and his family, and to make them a good home. A middle-aged servant had been living in the house for some days, and all was in preparation. Fires burnt in the grates, a leg of mutton smoked in the kitchen, and a canary in the living-room, which was immediately entered by the house door, sang a loud song of welcome.

'This, sir, will be our residence,' said Captain Jackman to the commander, who was staring agape and aghast around him, 'until we have stored some of the most secret of the hiding-places we have just passed with easily negotiable articles. I have taken you into my confidence, for you will not betray me. I do not fear death.' He smiled strangely as he looked at the commander. 'I must be a rich man, and Ada, my wife, and my love,' he exclaimed, turning a look of touching tenderness upon the girl, 'will share in my fortune, and possess it when I die. You can, if you choose, go away, and start the hounds of your own service after us. You will not do this. You will not, with your own hand, bring your son-in-law to the gallows.' The commander stared at him passionately, but in silence. He had long ago exhausted the language of horror. He had no further protests to offer against his son-in-law's daring scheme.

So nothing more was said in this way; and in the afternoon, at about two o'clock, when the leg of mutton had been eaten, Captain Jackman took a touching farewell of his wife. Again and again he pressed her to his heart. He gravely saluted the commander, not seeming then to have words for him. Where was he going? This madman—though, to be sure, it was still the age of the pirate, the smuggler, and the slaver—was bound away down the Portugal coast to intercept and plunder a large, rich ship which was sailing to the Indies on a date of which he had received private notice. The boat that had brought the party ashore lay in wait. He entered it, and was rowed aboard the brig, which lay at about a mile distant. Ada and the commander stood watching the vessel. The girl was too proud to weep before her father, and gazed haughtily at the picture on the sea. But what was happening there?

'Have you a glass?' almost shrieked the commander. 'By Heaven, Ada, I believe the men have seized the ship!'

Whilst he said it, the vessel was a scene

of commotion and disorder. A boat had
been lowered, and five men had pulled
hastily under the stern. The topsail had
been swung, then hauled afresh, and the
foretopsail backed, and within an hour of
Captain Jackman having gone on board his
ship to seize the Portuguese galleon, a boat
of the brig, with Bill Hoey steering her,
was swept to Bugsby's Hole.

Commander Conway and his daughter
ran down the tunnel to hear what had
happened. The huge form of Hoey stood
in the orifice, and beyond lay the boat in
the clear gleams and lights of the high
Atlantic afternoon, with men tending her,
and some gathering near to Hoey to listen
to what was to follow.

'I think you are a retired commander in
the Navy,' said Hoey, respectfully saluting
the commander.

'That's so. What's gone wrong with
you?' answered the commander, speaking
with great agitation.

'We want you to take charge of the brig
to a naval port, and tell our story for us,'
said Hoey. 'We was tricked into this job.

We never signed for piracy, and the likes of that. We was to seek for a treasure that lay hid in an island. We laid hold of him when he came aboard, and told him plainly that we had mutinied, and meant to carry the ship and himself to where we could report the case to an admiral. He knew we were no pirates. He turned black with passion. " Who's going to be answerable," says I, " for wrecking that there revenue cutter ?" He slapped his hand to his pocket, and I sprang upon him, and some of us ran him below, and locked him up in his own cabin. It has a big stern-window, which we had overlooked, and, being naturally mad, as all hands for some time had been aware, he goes and proves it by dropping overboard, and drowning himself, and I came off at once, sir, to give you the news, and ask for instructions.'

A long, wild shriek, incommunicable in words, rang through the tunnel, but Ada stood upright nevertheless.

' Are you sure he is drowned ?' asked the commander.

' Oh yes, sir,' answered Hoey. ' A good

search was made, and nothing of him was seen.'

'Oh, Walter!' moaned the girl; then, screaming at Hoey, 'Ruffians! cowards! murderers!' she swung on her heels, and rushed wildly up the tunnel.

'Ada,' shouted the commander after her, 'you will come along with us?'

'I will drown myself too, if you carry me on board,' she howled, just glancing round to say so; and she then went up the tunnel, and out of sight of them.

The commander knew his daughter; he was perfectly well aware that no entreaty was to move her. He lingered, considered, thought to himself, 'She has her home; when all this passion and grief have passed I will come down and take her away.' He entered the boat, but, in justice it must be said, with a most reluctant heart, and eyes which clung to the land.

And was our friend successful in courting his daughter out of the tremendous solitude of Bugsby's Hole? He knew that he stood no chance when the messenger, whom he had despatched to inquire after her, himself not choosing to be visible, returned with the information that it was believed by the simple adjacent villagers that she had lost her true bearings, and was, in fact, out of her course. This could be asserted, that every night, blow high or blow low, the poor, unhappy woman, whom her father never could persuade to abandon her wretched home, placed a lamp in a seaward-facing window.

THE END.

BILLING AND SONS, PRINTERS, GUILDFORD.

CHATTO & WINDUS'S
CHEAP POPULAR NOVELS
BY THE BEST AUTHORS.
Bound in Boards, TWO SHILLINGS each.

BY EDMOND ABOUT.
The Fellah.

BY HAMILTON AIDE.
Carr of Carrlyon.
Confidences.

BY MRS. ALEXANDER.
Maid, Wife, or Widow?
Valerie's Fate.
Blind Fate.
A Life Interest.
Mona's Choice.
By Woman's Wit.

BY GRANT ALLEN.
Strange Stories.
Philistia.
Babylon.
The Beckoning Hand.
In All Shades.
For Maimie's Sake.
The Devil's Die.
This Mortal Coil.
The Tents of Shem.
The Great Taboo.
Dumaresq's Daughter.
The Duchess of Powysland.
Blood Royal.
Ivan Greet's Masterpiece.
The Scallywag.
At Market Value.
Under Sealed Orders.

BY EDWIN LESTER ARNOLD.
Phra the Phœnician.

BY FRANK BARRETT.
A Recoiling Vengeance.
For Love and Honour.
John Ford ; and His Helpmate.
Honest Davie.
A Prodigal's Progress.
Folly Morrison.
Lieutenant Barnabas.
Found Guilty.
Fettered for Life.
Between Life and Death.
The Sin of Olga Zassoulich.
Little Lady Linton.

BY FRANK BARRETT—continued.
The Woman of the Iron Bracelets.
The Harding Scandal.
A Missing Witness.

BY SHELSLEY BEAUCHAMP,
Grantley Grange.

BY BESANT & RICE.
Ready-Money Mortiboy.
With Harp and Crown.
This Son of Vulcan.
My Little Girl.
The Case of Mr. Lucraft.
The Golden Butterfly.
By Celia's Arbour.
The Monks of Thelema.
'Twas in Trafalgar's Bay.
The Seamy Side.
The Ten Years' Tenant.
The Chaplain of the Fleet.

BY WALTER BESANT,
All Sorts and Conditions of Men.
The Captains' Room.
All in a Garden Fair.
Dorothy Forster.
Uncle Jack.
Children of Gibeon.
The World went very well then.
Herr Paulus.
For Faith and Freedom.
To Call her Mine.
The Bell of St. Paul's.
The Holy Rose.
Armorel of Lyonesse.
St. Katherine's by the Tower.
The Ivory Gate.
Verbena Camellia Stephanotis.
The Rebel Queen.
Beyond the Dreams of Avarice.
The Revolt of Man.
In Deacon's Orders.
The Master Craftsman.
The City of Refuge.

BY AMBROSE BIERCE.
In the Midst of Life.

London: CHATTO & WINDUS, 111 St. Martin's Lane, W.C.

BY FREDERICK BOYLE.
Camp Notes.
Savage Life.
Chronicles of No-Man's Land.

BY ROBERT BUCHANAN.
The Shadow of the Sword.
A Child of Nature.
God and the Man.
Annan Water.
The New Abelard.
The Martyrdom of Madeline.
Love Me for Ever.
Matt : a Story of a Caravan.
Foxglove Manor.
The Master of the Mine.
The Heir of Linne.
Woman and the Man.
Rachel Dene.
Lady Kilpatrick.

BY BUCHANAN AND MURRAY.
The Charlatan.

BY HALL CAINE.
The Shadow of a Crime.
A Son of Hagar.
The Deemster.

CY COMMANDER CAMERON.
The Cruise of the 'Black Prince.'

BY AUSTIN CLARE.
For the Love of a Lass.

BY MRS. ARCHER CLIVE.
Paul Ferroll.
Why Paul Ferroll Killed his Wife

BY MACLAREN COBBAN.
The Cure of Souls.
The Red Sultan.

BY C. ALLSTON COLLINS.
The Bar Sinister.

BY WILKIE COLLINS.
Armadale.
After Dark.
No Name.
A Rogue's Life.
Antonina. | Basil.
Hide and Seek.
The Dead Secret.
Queen of Hearts.
My Miscellanies.
The Woman in White.
The Moonstone.
Man and Wife.
Poor Miss Finch.

BY WILKIE COLLINS—*continued.*
Miss or Mrs. ?
The New Magdalen.
The Frozen Deep.
The Law and the Lady.
The Two Destinies.
The Haunted Hotel.
The Fallen Leaves.
Jezebel's Daughter.
The Black Robe.
Heart and Science.
'I say No.'
The Evil Genius.
Little Novels.
The Legacy of Cain.
Blind Love.

MORTIMER & FRANCES COLLINS.
Sweet Anne Page.
Transmigration.
From Midnight to Midnight.
A Fight with Fortune.
Sweet and Twenty.
Frances.
The Village Comedy.
You Play Me False.
Blacksmith and Scholar.

BY M. J. COLQUHOUN.
Every Inch a Soldier.

BY DUTTON COOK.
Paul Foster's Daughter.
Leo.

BY C. EGBERT CRADDOCK.
Prophet of the Smoky Mountains.

BY MATT CRIM.
Adventures of a Fair Rebel.

BY B. M. CROKER.
Pretty Miss Neville.
Proper Pride.
A Bird of Passage.
Diana Barrington.
'To Let.'
A Family Likeness.
Village Tales & Jungle Tragedies.
Two Masters.
Mr. Jervis.
The Real Lady Hilda.
Married or Single ?
Interference.
A Third Person.

BY WILLIAM CYPLES.
Hearts of Gold.

London : *CHATTO & WINDUS*, 111 *St. Martin's Lane*, *W.C.*

BY ALPHONSE DAUDET.
The Evangelist.

BY ERASMUS DAWSON.
The Fountain of Youth.

BY JAMES DE MILLE.
A Castle in Spain.

BY J. LEITH DERWENT.
Our Lady of Tears.
Circe's Lovers.

BY DICK DONOVAN.
The Man-hunter.
Caught at Last!
Tracked and Taken.
Who Poisoned Hetty Duncan?
The Man from Manchester.
A Detective's Triumphs.
In the Grip of the Law.
Wanted!
From Information Received.
Tracked to Doom.
Link by Link.
Suspicion Aroused.
Dark Deeds.
Riddles Read.
The Mystery of Jamaica Terrace.
Chronicles of Michael Danevitch.

BY MRS. ANNIE EDWARDES.
A Point of Honour.
Archie Lovell.

BY M. BETHAM-EDWARDS.
Felicia.
Kitty.

BY EDWARD EGGLESTON.
Roxy.

BY G. MANVILLE FENN.
The New Mistress.
Witness to the Deed.
The Tiger Lily.
The White Virgin.

BY PERCY FITZGERALD.
Bella Donna.
Polly.
The Second Mrs. Tillotson.
Seventy-five Brooke Street.
Never Forgotten.
The Lady of Brantome.
Fatal Zero.

BY PERCY FITZGERALD and Others.
Strange Secrets.

BY ALBANY DE FONBLANQUE.
Filthy Lucre.

BY R. E. FRANCILLON.
Olympia.
One by One.
Queen Cophetua.
A Real Queen.
King or Knave.
Romances of the Law.
Ropes of Sand.
A Dog and his Shadow.

BY HAROLD FREDERIC.
Seth's Brother's Wife.
The Lawton Girl.

Prefaced by Sir H. BARTLE FRERE.
Pandurang Hàrì.

BY EDWARD GARRETT.
The Capel Girls.

BY GILBERT GAUL.
A Strange Manuscript.

BY CHARLES GIBBON.
Robin Gray.
For Lack of Gold.
What will the World Say?
In Honour Bound.
In Love and War.
For the King.
Queen of the Meadow.
In Pastures Green.
The Flower of the Forest.
A Heart's Problem.
The Braes of Yarrow.
The Golden Shaft.
Of High Degree.
The Dead Heart.
By Mead and Stream.
Heart's Delight.
Fancy Free.
Loving a Dream.
A Hard Knot.
Blood-Money.

BY WILLIAM GILBERT.
James Duke.
Dr. Austin's Guests.
The Wizard of the Mountain.

London: CHATTO & WINDUS, 111 *St. Martin's Lane, W.C.*

BY ERNEST GLANVILLE.
The Lost Heiress.
The Fossicker.
A Fair Colonist.

BY REV. S. BARING GOULD.
Eve.
Red Spider.

BY HENRY GREVILLE.
Nikanor.
A Noble Woman.

BY CECIL GRIFFITH.
Corinthia Marazion.

BY SYDNEY GRUNDY.
The Days of his Vanity.

BY JOHN HABBERTON.
Brueton's Bayou.
Country Luck.

BY ANDREW HALLIDAY.
Every-Day Papers.

BY THOMAS HARDY.
Under the Greenwood Tree.

BY BRET HARTE.
An Heiress of Red Dog.
The Luck of Roaring Camp.
Californian Stories.
Gabriel Conroy.
Flip.
Maruja.
A Phyllis of the Sierras.
A Waif of the Plains.
A Ward of the Golden Gate.

BY JULIAN HAWTHORNE.
Garth.
Ellice Quentin.
Sebastian Strome.
Dust.
Fortune's Fool.
Beatrix Randolph.
Miss Cadogna.
Love—or a Name.
D. Poindexter's Disappearance.
The Spectre of the Camera.

BY SIR ARTHUR HELPS.
Ivan de Biron.

BY G. A. HENTY.
Rujub, the Juggler.

BY HENRY HERMAN.
A Leading Lady.

BY HEADON HILL.
Zambra, the Detective.

BY JOHN HILL.
Treason-Felony.

BY MRS. CASHEL HOEY.
The Lover's Creed.

BY MRS. GEORGE HOOPER.
The House of Raby.

BY MRS. HUNGERFORD.
In Durance Vile.
A Maiden all Forlorn.
A Mental Struggle.
Marvel.
A Modern Circe.
Lady Verner's Flight.
The Red-House Mystery.
The Three Graces.
An Unsatisfactory Lover.
Lady Patty.
Nora Creina.
April's Lady.
Peter's Wife.
The Professor's Experiment.

BY MRS. ALFRED HUNT.
Thornicroft's Model.
The Leaden Casket.
Self-Condemned.
That Other Person.

BY WILLIAM JAMESON.
My Dead Self.

BY HARRIETT JAY.
The Dark Colleen.
The Queen of Connaught.

BY MARK KERSHAW.
Colonial Facts and Fictions.

BY R. ASHE KING.
A Drawn Game.
'The Wearing of the Green.'
Passion's Slave.
Bell Barry.

BY EDMOND LEPELLETIER.
Madame Sans-Gêne.

London: CHATTO & WINDUS, 111 St. Martin's Lane, W.C.

BY JOHN LEYS.
The Lindsays.

BY E. LYNN LINTON.
Patricia Kemball.
The Atonement of Leam Dundas.
The World Well Lost.
Under which Lord?
With a Silken Thread.
The Rebel of the Family.
'My Love!'
Ione.
Paston Carew.
Sowing the Wind.
The One too Many.
Dulcie Everton.

BY HENRY W. LUCY.
Gideon Fleyce.

BY JUSTIN McCARTHY.
Dear Lady Disdain.
The Waterdale Neighbours.
My Enemy's Daughter.
A Fair Saxon.
Linley Rochford.
Miss Misanthrope.
Donna Quixote.
The Comet of a Season.
Maid of Athens.
Camiola: a Girl with a Fortune.
The Dictator.
Red Diamonds.
The Riddle Ring.

BY HUGH MacCOLL.
Mr. Stranger's Sealed Packet.

BY GEORGE MACDONALD.
Heather and Snow.

BY MRS. MACDONELL.
Quaker Cousins.

BY KATHARINE S. MACQUOID.
The Evil Eye.
Lost Rose.

BY W. H. MALLOCK.
The New Republic.
A Romance of the 19th Century.

BY J. MASTERMAN.
Half-a-dozen Daughters.

BY BRANDER MATTHEWS.
A Secret of the Sea.

BY L. T. MEADE.
A Soldier of Fortune.

BY LEONARD MERRICK.
The Man who was Good.

BY JEAN MIDDLEMASS.
Touch and Go.
Mr. Dorillion.

BY MRS. MOLESWORTH.
Hathercourt Rectory.

BY J. E. MUDDOCK.
Stories Weird and Wonderful.
The Dead Man's Secret.
From the Bosom of the Deep.

BY D. CHRISTIE MURRAY.
A Life's Atonement.
Joseph's Coat.
Val Strange.
A Model Father.
Coals of Fire.
Hearts.
By the Gate of the Sea.
The Way of the World.
A Bit of Human Nature.
First Person Singular.
Cynic Fortune.
Old Blazer's Hero.
Bob Martin's Little Girl.
Time's Revenges.
A Wasted Crime.
In Direst Peril.
Mount Despair.
A Capful o' Nails.

BY MURRAY AND HERMAN.
One Traveller Returns.
Paul Jones's Alias.
The Bishops' Bible.

BY HENRY MURRAY.
A Game of Bluff.
A Song of Sixpence.

BY HUME NISBET.
'Bail Up!'
Dr. Bernard St. Vincent.

BY W. E. NORRIS.
Saint Ann's.
Billy Bellew.

BY ALICE O'HANLON.
The Unforeseen.
Chance? or Fate?

London: CHATTO & WINDUS, 111 St. Martin's Lane, W.C.

BY GEORGES OHNET.
Doctor Rameau.
A Last Love.
A Weird Gift.

BY MRS. OLIPHANT.
Whiteladies.
The Primrose Path.
The Greatest Heiress in England

BY MRS. ROBERT O'REILLY.
Phœbe's Fortunes.

BY OUIDA.
Held in Bondage.
Strathmore.
Chandos.
Under Two Flags.
Idalia.
Cecil Castlemaine's Gage.
Tricotrin.
Puck.
Folle Farine.
A Dog of Flanders.
Pascarèl.
Signa.
In a Winter City.
Ariadnê.
Moths.
Friendship.
Pipistrello.
Bimbi.
In Maremma.
Wanda.
Frescoes.
Princess Napraxine.
Two Little Wooden Shoes.
A Village Commune.
Othmar.
Guilderoy.
Ruffino.
Syrlin.
Santa Barbara.
Two Offenders.
Wisdom, Wit, and Pathos.

BY MARGARET AGNES PAUL.
Gentle and Simple.

BY JAMES PAYN.
Lost Sir Massingberd.
A Perfect Treasure.
Bentinck's Tutor.
Murphy's Master.
A County Family

BY JAMES PAYN—*continued.*
At Her Mercy.
A Woman's Vengeance.
Cecil's Tryst.
The Clyffards of Clyffe.
The Family Scapegrace.
The Foster Brothers.
The Best of Husbands.
Found Dead.
Walter's Word.
Halves.
Fallen Fortunes.
What He Cost Her.
Humorous Stories.
Gwendoline's Harvest.
Like Father, Like Son.
A Marine Residence.
Married Beneath Him.
Mirk Abbey.
Not Wooed, but Won.
Two Hundred Pounds Reward.
Less Black than We're Painted.
By Proxy.
High Spirits.
Under One Roof.
Carlyon's Year.
A Confidential Agent.
Some Private Views.
A Grape from a Thorn.
From Exile.
Kit: A Memory.
For Cash Only.
The Canon's Ward.
The Talk of the Town.
Holiday Tasks.
Glow-worm Tales.
The Mystery of Mirbridge.
The Burnt Million.
The Word and the Will.
A Prince of the Blood.
Sunny Stories.
A Trying Patient.

BY EDGAR A. POE.
The Mystery of Marie Roget.

BY MRS. CAMPBELL PRAED.
The Romance of a Station.
The Soul of Countess Adrian.
Outlaw and Lawmaker.
Christina Chard.
Mrs. Tregaskiss.

London: CHATTO & WINDUS, 111 *St. Martin's Lane,* W.C.

BY E. C. PRICE.
Valentina.
Gerald.
Mrs. Lancaster's Rival.
The Foreigners.
BY RICHARD PRYCE.
Miss Maxwell's Affections.
BY CHARLES READE.
It is Never Too Late to Mend.
Hard Cash.
Peg Woffington.
Christie Johnstone.
Griffith Gaunt.
Put Yourself in His Place.
The Double Marriage.
Love Me Little, Love Me Long.
Foul Play.
The Cloister and the Hearth.
The Course of True Love.
The Autobiography of a Thief.
A Terrible Temptation.
The Wandering Heir.
A Simpleton.
A Woman-Hater.
Singleheart and Doubleface.
Good Stories of Man and other
The Jilt.   [Animals.
A Perilous Secret.
Readiana.
BY MRS. J. H. RIDDELL.
Her Mother's Darling.
The Uninhabited House.
Weird Stories.
Fairy Water.
Prince of Wales's Garden Party.
The Mystery in Palace Gardens.
The Nun's Curse.
Idle Tales.
BY AMÉLIE RIVES.
Barbara Dering.
BY F. W. ROBINSON.
Women are Strange.
The Hands of Justice.
The Woman in the Dark.
BY JAMES RUNCIMAN.
Skippers and Shellbacks.
Grace Balmaign's Sweetheart.
Schools and Scholars.
BY DORA RUSSELL.
A Country Sweetheart.

BY W. CLARK RUSSELL.
Round the Galley Fire.
On the Fo'k'sle Head.
In the Middle Watch.
A Voyage to the Cape.
A Book for the Hammock.
Mystery of the 'Ocean Star.'
The Romance of Jenny Harlowe.
An Ocean Tragedy.
My Shipmate Louise.
Alone on a Wide Wide Sea.
The Phantom Death.
The Good Ship 'Mohock.'
Is He the Man?
Heart of Oak.
The Convict Ship.
The Tale of the Ten.
The Last Entry.
BY ALAN ST. AUBYN.
A Fellow of Trinity.
The Junior Dean.
The Master of St. Benedict's.
To His Own Master.
Orchard Damerel.
In the Face of the World.
The Tremlett Diamonds.
BY GEORGE AUGUSTUS SALA.
Gaslight and Daylight.
BY GEORGE R. SIMS.
The Ring o' Bells.
Mary Jane's Memoirs.
Mary Jane Married.
Tales of To-day.
Dramas of Life.
Tinkletop's Crime.
Zeph: a Circus Story.
My Two Wives.
Memoirs of a Landlady.
Scenes from the Show.
The Ten Commandments.
Dagonet Abroad.
Rogues and Vagabonds.
BY ARTHUR SKETCHLEY.
A Match in the Dark.
BY HAWLEY SMART.
Without Love or Licence.
The Plunger.
Beatrice and Benedick.
Long Odds.
The Master of Rathkelly.

London: CHATTO & WINDUS, 111 St. Martin's Lane, W.C.

BY T. W. SPEIGHT.
The Mysteries of Heron Dyke.
The Golden Hoop.
By Devious Ways.
Hoodwinked.
Back to Life.
The Loudwater Tragedy.
Burgo's Romance.
Quittance in Full.
A Husband from the Sea.

BY R. A. STERNDALE.
The Afghan Knife.

BY R. LOUIS STEVENSON.
New Arabian Nights.

BY BERTHA THOMAS.
Proud Maisie.
The Violin-player.
Cressida.

BY WALTER THORNBURY.
Tales for the Marines.
Old Stories Re-told.

BY ANTHONY TROLLOPE.
The Way We Live Now.
Mr. Scarborough's Family.
The Golden Lion of Granpère.
The American Senator.
Frau Frohmann.
Marion Fay.
Kept in the Dark.
The Land-Leaguers.
John Caldigate.

BY FRANCES E. TROLLOPE.
Anne Furness.
Mabel's Progress.
Like Ships upon the Sea.

BY T. ADOLPHUS TROLLOPE.
Diamond Cut Diamond.

BY J. T. TROWBRIDGE.
Farnell's Folly.

BY IVAN TURGENIEFF, etc.
Stories from Foreign Novelists.

BY MARK TWAIN.
Tom Sawyer.
A Tramp Abroad.
The Stolen White Elephant.
Pleasure Trip on the Continent.

BY MARK TWAIN—continued.
The Gilded Age.
Huckleberry Finn.
Life on the Mississippi.
The Prince and the Pauper.
Mark Twain's Sketches.
Yankee at Court of K. Arthur.
The £1,000,000 Bank-note.

BY SARAH TYTLER.
Noblesse Oblige.
Citoyenne Jacqueline.
The Huguenot Family.
What She Came Through.
Beauty and the Beast.
The Bride's Pass.
Saint Mungo's City.
Disappeared.
Lady Bell.
Buried Diamonds.
The Blackhall Ghosts.

BY C. C. FRASER-TYTLER.
Mistress Judith.

BY ALLEN UPWARD.
The Queen against Owen.
The Prince of Balkistan.

BY ARTEMUS WARD.
Artemus Ward Complete.

BY AARON WATSON AND LILLIAS WASSERMANN.
The Marquis of Carabas.

BY WILLIAM WESTALL.
Trust-Money.

BY MRS. F. H. WILLIAMSON.
A Child Widow.

BY J. S. WINTER.
Cavalry Life.
Regimental Legends.

BY H. F. WOOD.
Passenger from Scotland Yard.
Englishman of the Rue Cain.

BY CELIA PARKER WOOLLEY.
Rachel Armstrong.

BY EDMUND YATES.
Castaway.
Land at Last.
The Forlorn Hope.

London: CHATTO & WINDUS, 111 St. Martin's Lane, W.C.

www.ingramcontent.com/pod-product-compliance
Lightning Source LLC
Chambersburg PA
CBHW020628030726
47497CB00007B/2466